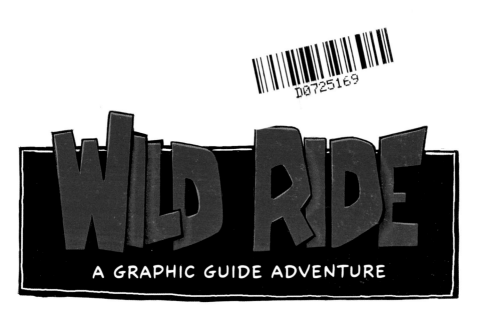

WILD RIDE

A GRAPHIC GUIDE ADVENTURE

WRITTEN BY
LIAM O'DONNELL

ILLUSTRATED BY
MIKE DEAS

ORCA BOOK PUBLISHERS

Library and Archives Canada Cataloguing in Publication

O'Donnell, Liam, 1970-
Wild ride / written by Liam O'Donnell ; illustrated by Michael Deas.

ISBN 978-1-55143-756-9

1. Survival after airplane accidents, shipwrecks, etc.--Juvenile fiction.
2. Survival skills--Juvenile fiction. I. Deas, Michael, 1982- II. Title.

PN6733.O36W54 2007   jC813'.6   C2007-902428-9

First published in the United States, 2007

Library of Congress Control Number: 2007926445

Summary: Devin, Nadia and Marcus are lost in the woods in a struggle for survival.
In graphic novel form.

Orca Book Publishers gratefully acknowledges the support for its publishing programs provided
by the following agencies: the Government of Canada through the Book Publishing Industry
Development Program and the Canada Council for the Arts, and the Province of British Columbia
through the BC Arts Council and the Book Publishing Tax Credit.

Cover and interior artwork by Mike Deas
Cover layout by Teresa Bubela
Author photo by Melanie McBride
Illustrator photo by Ellen Ho

ORCA BOOK PUBLISHERS
PO Box 5626, STN. B
VICTORIA, BC CANADA
V8R 6S4

ORCA BOOK PUBLISHERS
PO Box 468
CUSTER, WA USA
98240-0468

www.orcabook.com
Printed and bound in China.

11 10 09 08 • 6 5 4 3

CHAPTER ONE
INTO THE WILD

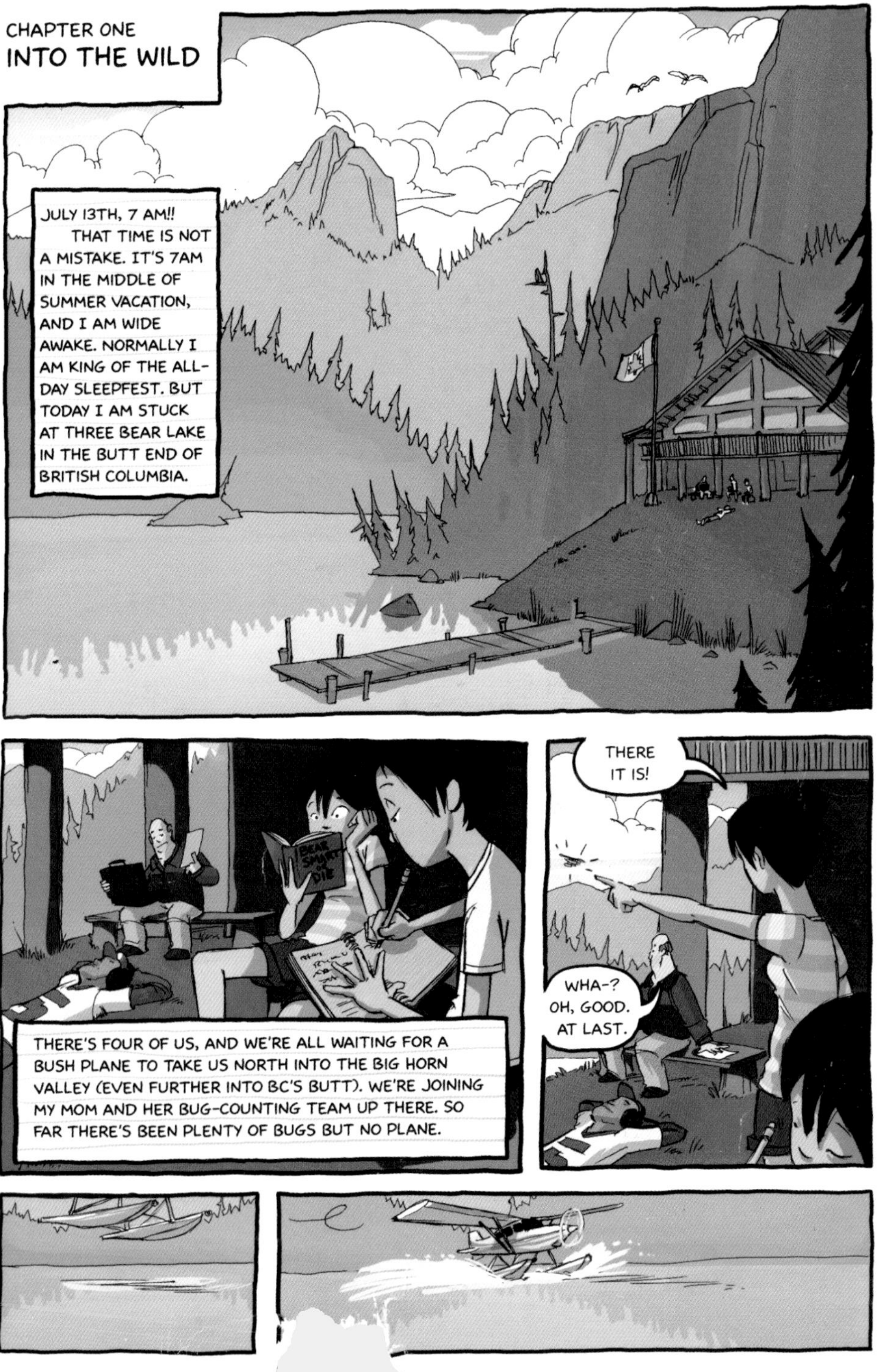
JULY 13TH, 7 AM!!
THAT TIME IS NOT A MISTAKE. IT'S 7AM IN THE MIDDLE OF SUMMER VACATION, AND I AM WIDE AWAKE. NORMALLY I AM KING OF THE ALL-DAY SLEEPFEST. BUT TODAY I AM STUCK AT THREE BEAR LAKE IN THE BUTT END OF BRITISH COLUMBIA.
THERE'S FOUR OF US, AND WE'RE ALL WAITING FOR A BUSH PLANE TO TAKE US NORTH INTO THE BIG HORN VALLEY (EVEN FURTHER INTO BC'S BUTT). WE'RE JOINING MY MOM AND HER BUG-COUNTING TEAM UP THERE. SO FAR THERE'S BEEN PLENTY OF BUGS BUT NO PLANE.
THERE IT IS!
WHA-? OH, GOOD. AT LAST.

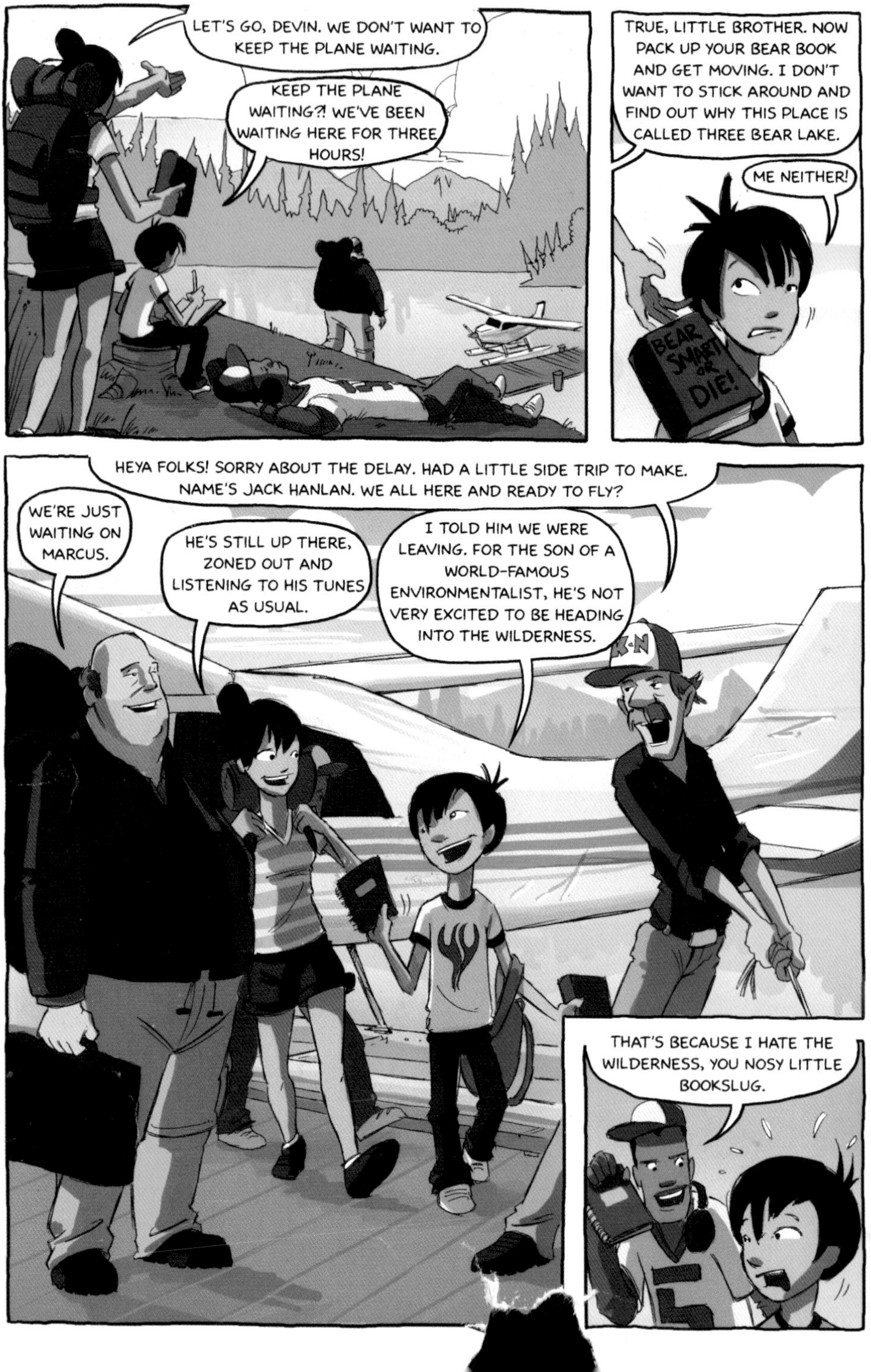

LET'S GO, DEVIN. WE DON'T WANT TO KEEP THE PLANE WAITING.
KEEP THE PLANE WAITING?! WE'VE BEEN WAITING HERE FOR THREE HOURS!
TRUE, LITTLE BROTHER. NOW PACK UP YOUR BEAR BOOK AND GET MOVING. I DON'T WANT TO STICK AROUND AND FIND OUT WHY THIS PLACE IS CALLED THREE BEAR LAKE.
ME NEITHER!
BEAR SMART OR DIE!
HEYA FOLKS! SORRY ABOUT THE DELAY. HAD A LITTLE SIDE TRIP TO MAKE. NAME'S JACK HANLAN. WE ALL HERE AND READY TO FLY?
WE'RE JUST WAITING ON MARCUS.
HE'S STILL UP THERE, ZONED OUT AND LISTENING TO HIS TUNES AS USUAL.
I TOLD HIM WE WERE LEAVING. FOR THE SON OF A WORLD-FAMOUS ENVIRONMENTALIST, HE'S NOT VERY EXCITED TO BE HEADING INTO THE WILDERNESS.
THAT'S BECAUSE I HATE THE WILDERNESS, YOU NOSY LITTLE BOOKSLUG.

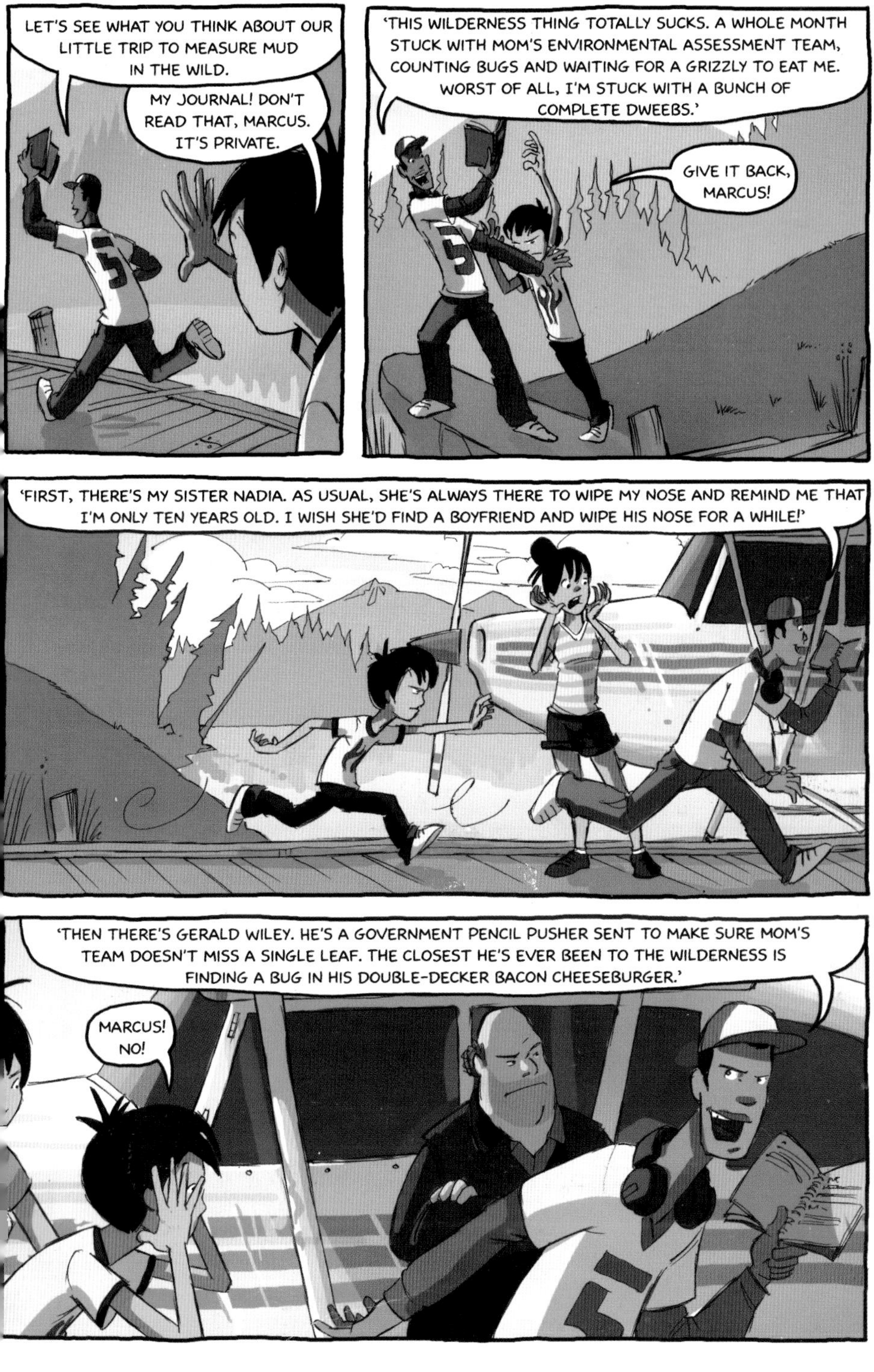
LET'S SEE WHAT YOU THINK ABOUT OUR LITTLE TRIP TO MEASURE MUD IN THE WILD.
MY JOURNAL! DON'T READ THAT, MARCUS. IT'S PRIVATE.
'THIS WILDERNESS THING TOTALLY SUCKS. A WHOLE MONTH STUCK WITH MOM'S ENVIRONMENTAL ASSESSMENT TEAM, COUNTING BUGS AND WAITING FOR A GRIZZLY TO EAT ME. WORST OF ALL, I'M STUCK WITH A BUNCH OF COMPLETE DWEEBS.'
GIVE IT BACK, MARCUS!
'FIRST, THERE'S MY SISTER NADIA. AS USUAL, SHE'S ALWAYS THERE TO WIPE MY NOSE AND REMIND ME THAT I'M ONLY TEN YEARS OLD. I WISH SHE'D FIND A BOYFRIEND AND WIPE HIS NOSE FOR A WHILE!'
'THEN THERE'S GERALD WILEY. HE'S A GOVERNMENT PENCIL PUSHER SENT TO MAKE SURE MOM'S TEAM DOESN'T MISS A SINGLE LEAF. THE CLOSEST HE'S EVER BEEN TO THE WILDERNESS IS FINDING A BUG IN HIS DOUBLE-DECKER BACON CHEESEBURGER.'
MARCUS! NO!

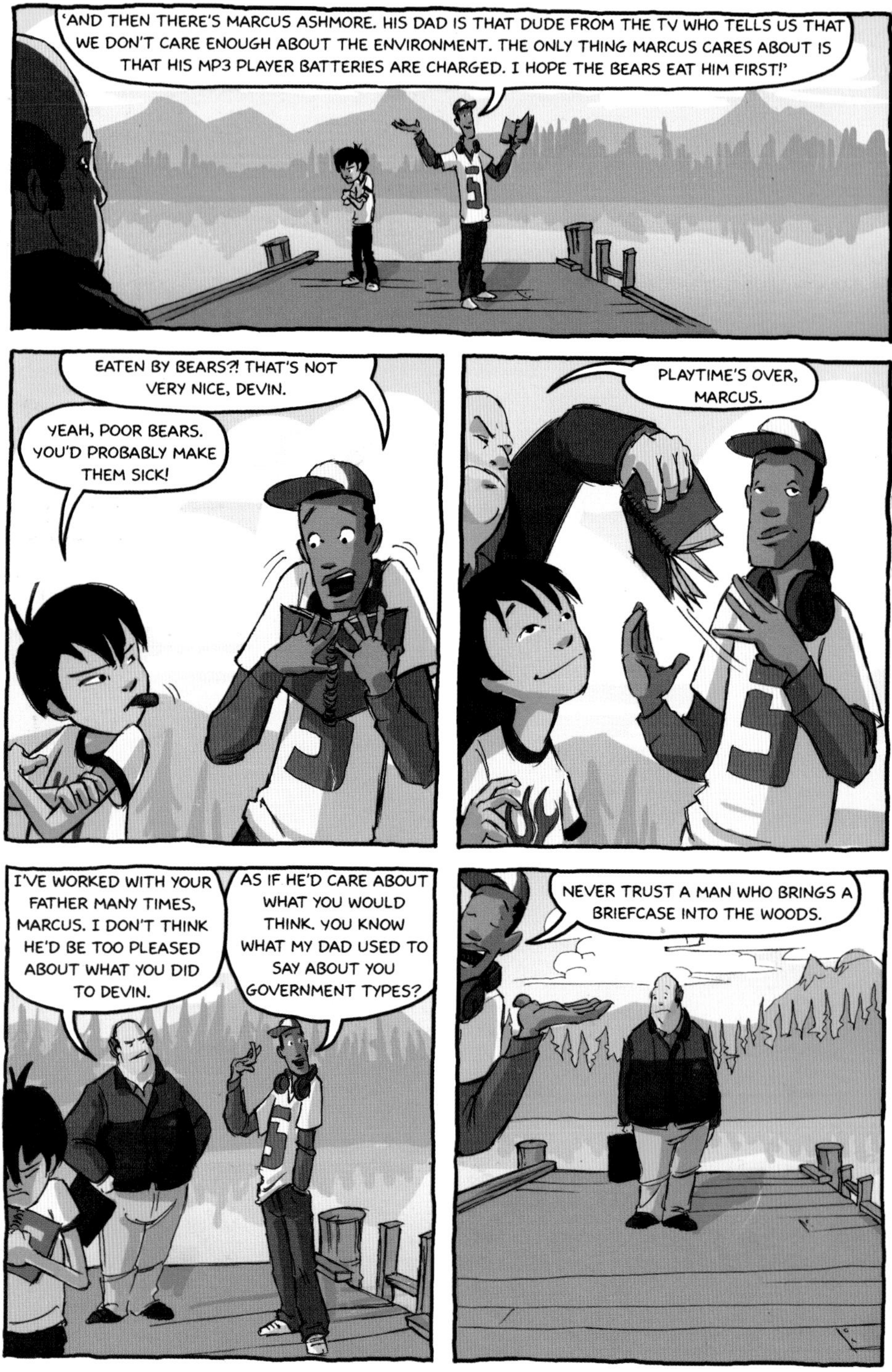
'AND THEN THERE'S MARCUS ASHMORE. HIS DAD IS THAT DUDE FROM THE TV WHO TELLS US THAT WE DON'T CARE ENOUGH ABOUT THE ENVIRONMENT. THE ONLY THING MARCUS CARES ABOUT IS THAT HIS MP3 PLAYER BATTERIES ARE CHARGED. I HOPE THE BEARS EAT HIM FIRST!'
EATEN BY BEARS?! THAT'S NOT VERY NICE, DEVIN.
YEAH, POOR BEARS. YOU'D PROBABLY MAKE THEM SICK!
PLAYTIME'S OVER, MARCUS.
I'VE WORKED WITH YOUR FATHER MANY TIMES, MARCUS. I DON'T THINK HE'D BE TOO PLEASED ABOUT WHAT YOU DID TO DEVIN.
AS IF HE'D CARE ABOUT WHAT YOU WOULD THINK. YOU KNOW WHAT MY DAD USED TO SAY ABOUT YOU GOVERNMENT TYPES?
NEVER TRUST A MAN WHO BRINGS A BRIEFCASE INTO THE WOODS.

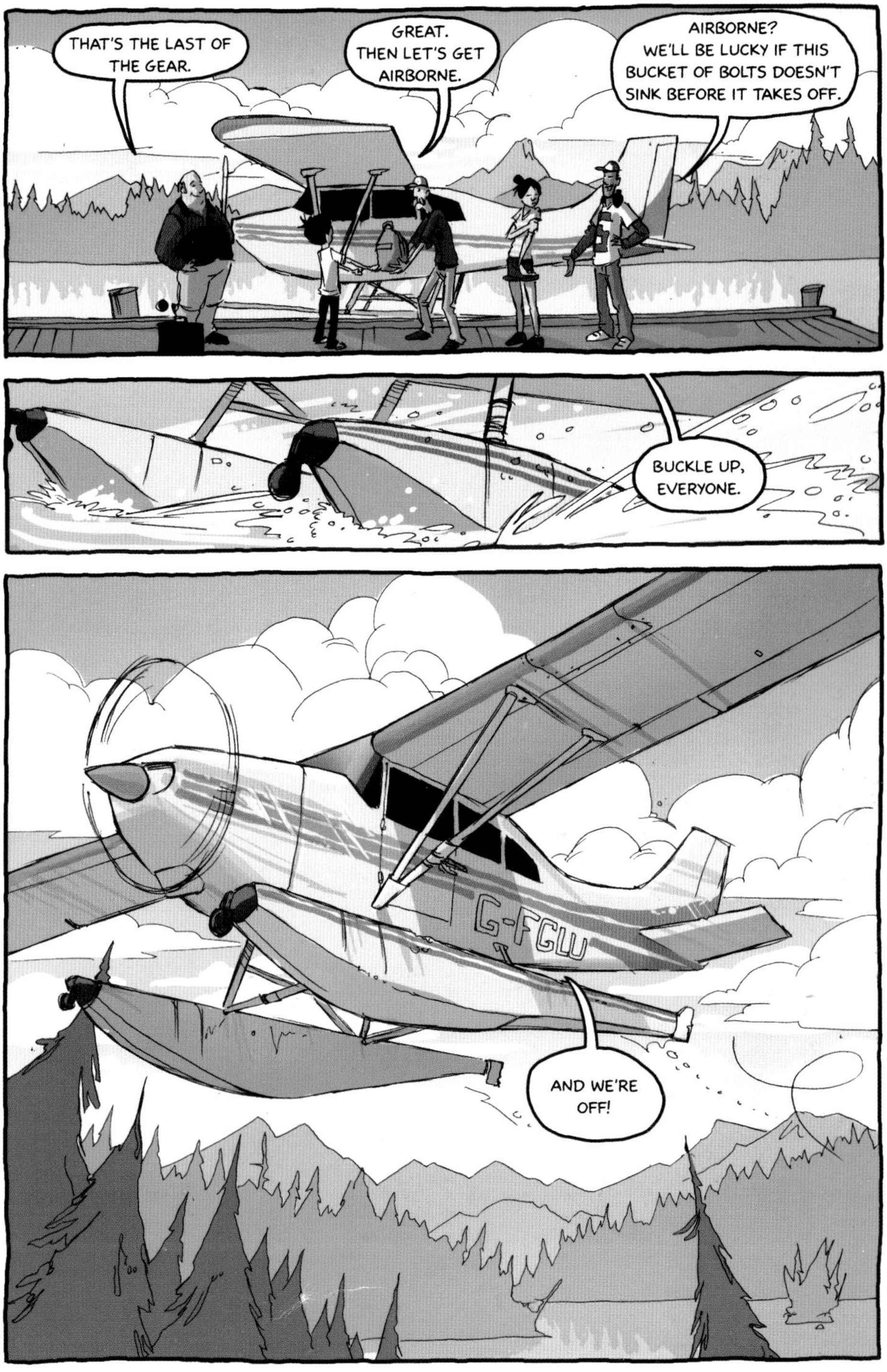
THAT'S THE LAST OF THE GEAR.
GREAT. THEN LET'S GET AIRBORNE.
AIRBORNE? WE'LL BE LUCKY IF THIS BUCKET OF BOLTS DOESN'T SINK BEFORE IT TAKES OFF.
BUCKLE UP, EVERYONE.
G-FGLU
AND WE'RE OFF!

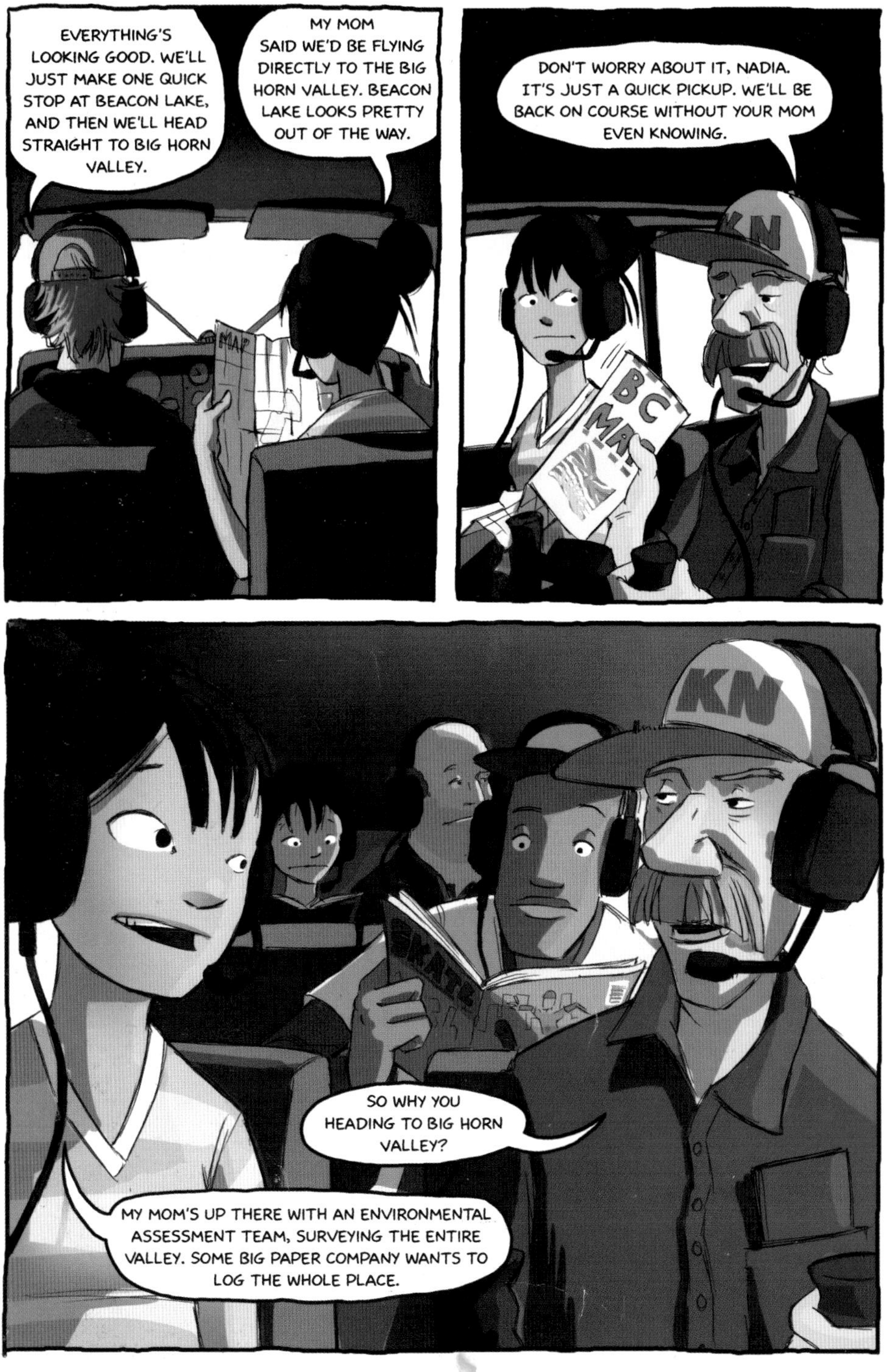
EVERYTHING'S LOOKING GOOD. WE'LL JUST MAKE ONE QUICK STOP AT BEACON LAKE, AND THEN WE'LL HEAD STRAIGHT TO BIG HORN VALLEY.
MY MOM SAID WE'D BE FLYING DIRECTLY TO THE BIG HORN VALLEY. BEACON LAKE LOOKS PRETTY OUT OF THE WAY.
MAP
DON'T WORRY ABOUT IT, NADIA. IT'S JUST A QUICK PICKUP. WE'LL BE BACK ON COURSE WITHOUT YOUR MOM EVEN KNOWING.
KN
BC
KN
SO WHY YOU HEADING TO BIG HORN VALLEY?
MY MOM'S UP THERE WITH AN ENVIRONMENTAL ASSESSMENT TEAM, SURVEYING THE ENTIRE VALLEY. SOME BIG PAPER COMPANY WANTS TO LOG THE WHOLE PLACE.

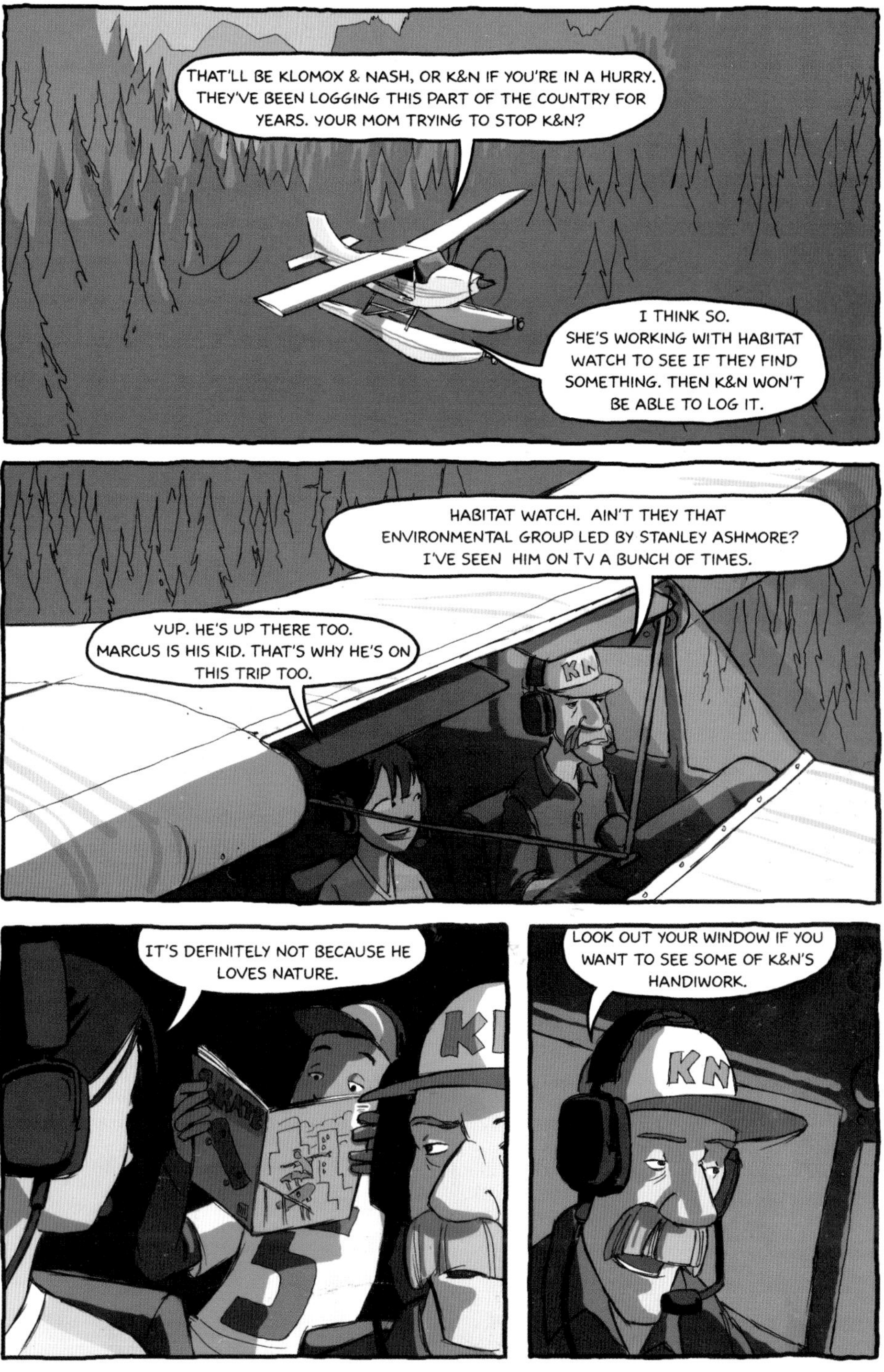
THAT'LL BE KLOMOX & NASH, OR K&N IF YOU'RE IN A HURRY. THEY'VE BEEN LOGGING THIS PART OF THE COUNTRY FOR YEARS. YOUR MOM TRYING TO STOP K&N?
I THINK SO. SHE'S WORKING WITH HABITAT WATCH TO SEE IF THEY FIND SOMETHING. THEN K&N WON'T BE ABLE TO LOG IT.
HABITAT WATCH. AIN'T THEY THAT ENVIRONMENTAL GROUP LED BY STANLEY ASHMORE? I'VE SEEN HIM ON TV A BUNCH OF TIMES.
YUP. HE'S UP THERE TOO. MARCUS IS HIS KID. THAT'S WHY HE'S ON THIS TRIP TOO.
K N
IT'S DEFINITELY NOT BECAUSE HE LOVES NATURE.
LOOK OUT YOUR WINDOW IF YOU WANT TO SEE SOME OF K&N'S HANDIWORK.
K N

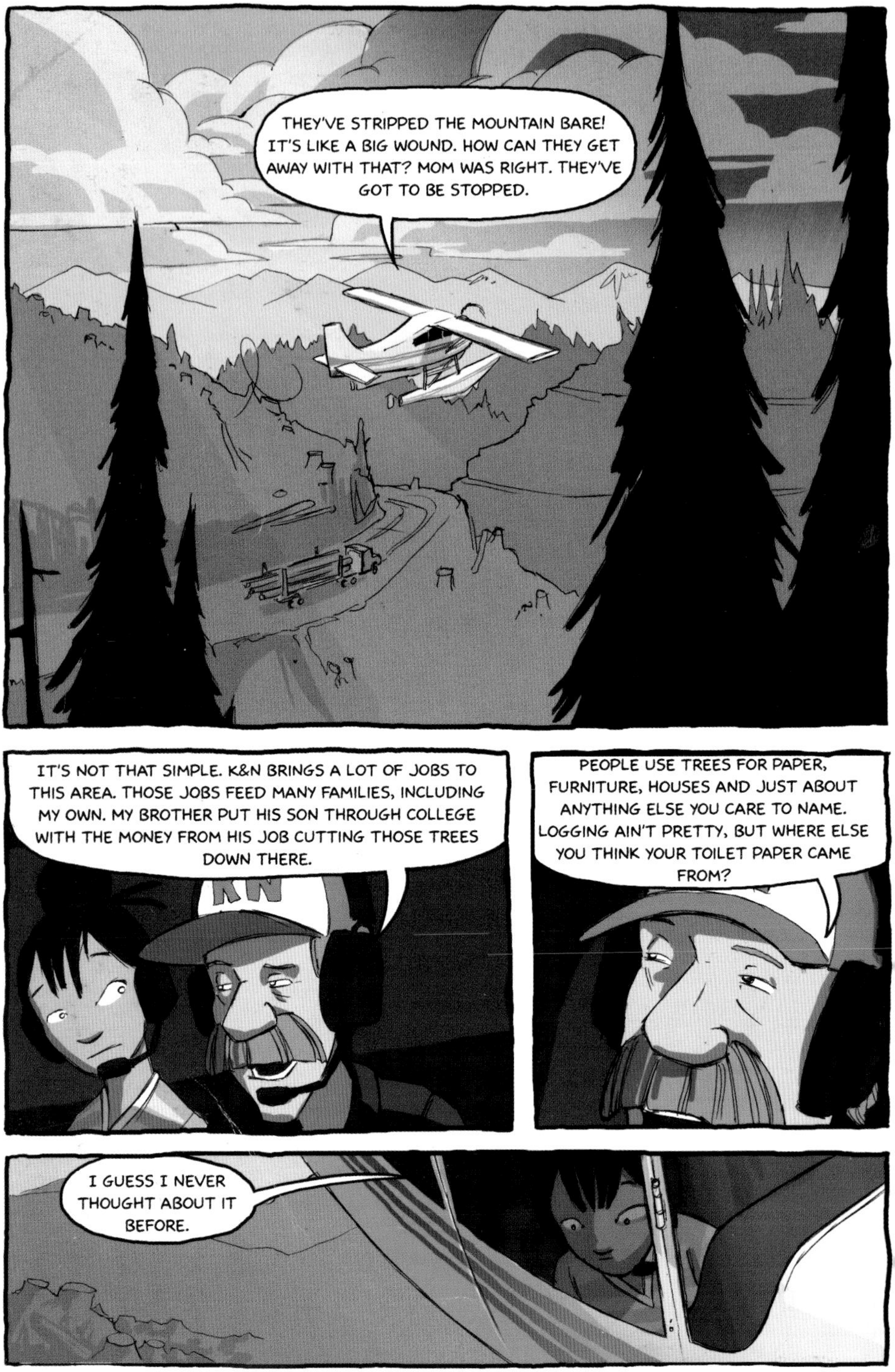
THEY'VE STRIPPED THE MOUNTAIN BARE! IT'S LIKE A BIG WOUND. HOW CAN THEY GET AWAY WITH THAT? MOM WAS RIGHT. THEY'VE GOT TO BE STOPPED.
IT'S NOT THAT SIMPLE. K&N BRINGS A LOT OF JOBS TO THIS AREA. THOSE JOBS FEED MANY FAMILIES, INCLUDING MY OWN. MY BROTHER PUT HIS SON THROUGH COLLEGE WITH THE MONEY FROM HIS JOB CUTTING THOSE TREES DOWN THERE.
KN
PEOPLE USE TREES FOR PAPER, FURNITURE, HOUSES AND JUST ABOUT ANYTHING ELSE YOU CARE TO NAME. LOGGING AIN'T PRETTY, BUT WHERE ELSE YOU THINK YOUR TOILET PAPER CAME FROM?
I GUESS I NEVER THOUGHT ABOUT IT BEFORE.

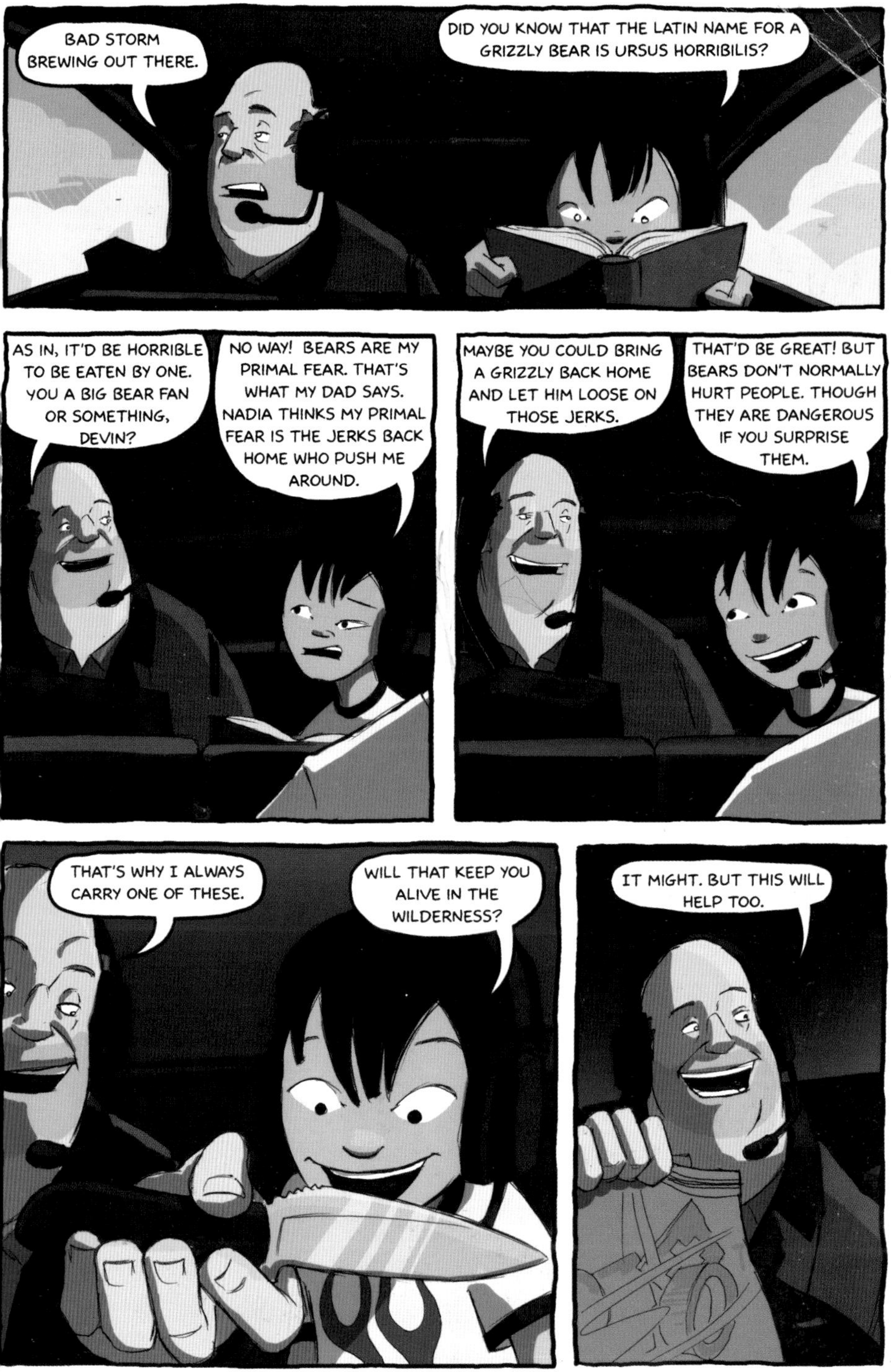
BAD STORM BREWING OUT THERE.
DID YOU KNOW THAT THE LATIN NAME FOR A GRIZZLY BEAR IS URSUS HORRIBILIS?
AS IN, IT'D BE HORRIBLE TO BE EATEN BY ONE. YOU A BIG BEAR FAN OR SOMETHING, DEVIN?
NO WAY! BEARS ARE MY PRIMAL FEAR. THAT'S WHAT MY DAD SAYS. NADIA THINKS MY PRIMAL FEAR IS THE JERKS BACK HOME WHO PUSH ME AROUND.
MAYBE YOU COULD BRING A GRIZZLY BACK HOME AND LET HIM LOOSE ON THOSE JERKS.
THAT'D BE GREAT! BUT BEARS DON'T NORMALLY HURT PEOPLE. THOUGH THEY ARE DANGEROUS IF YOU SURPRISE THEM.
THAT'S WHY I ALWAYS CARRY ONE OF THESE.
WILL THAT KEEP YOU ALIVE IN THE WILDERNESS?
IT MIGHT. BUT THIS WILL HELP TOO.

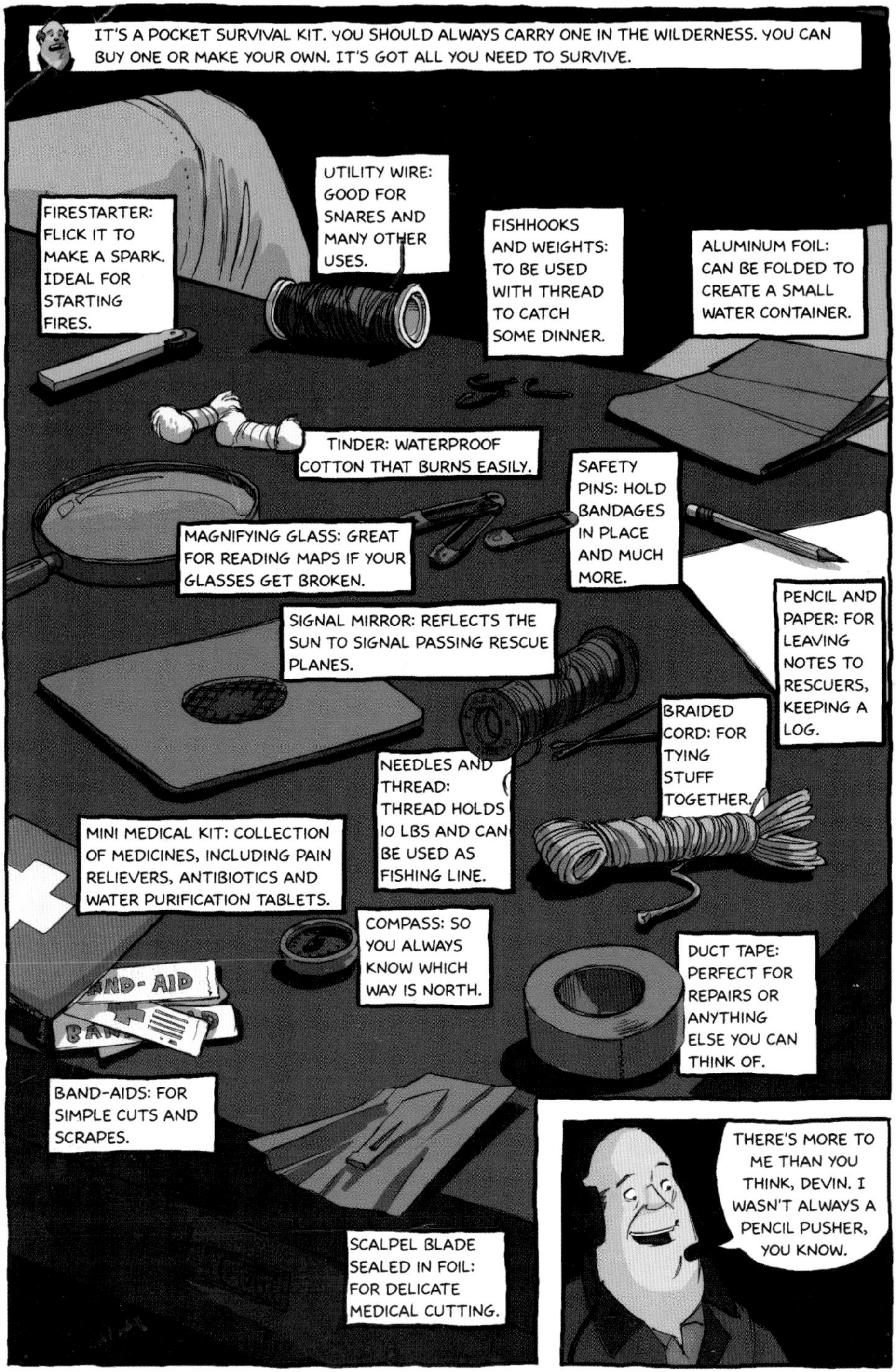

IT'S A POCKET SURVIVAL KIT. YOU SHOULD ALWAYS CARRY ONE IN THE WILDERNESS. YOU CAN BUY ONE OR MAKE YOUR OWN. IT'S GOT ALL YOU NEED TO SURVIVE.
FIRESTARTER: FLICK IT TO MAKE A SPARK. IDEAL FOR STARTING FIRES.
UTILITY WIRE: GOOD FOR SNARES AND MANY OTHER USES.
FISHHOOKS AND WEIGHTS: TO BE USED WITH THREAD TO CATCH SOME DINNER.
ALUMINUM FOIL: CAN BE FOLDED TO CREATE A SMALL WATER CONTAINER.
TINDER: WATERPROOF COTTON THAT BURNS EASILY.
SAFETY PINS: HOLD BANDAGES IN PLACE AND MUCH MORE.
MAGNIFYING GLASS: GREAT FOR READING MAPS IF YOUR GLASSES GET BROKEN.
PENCIL AND PAPER: FOR LEAVING NOTES TO RESCUERS, KEEPING A LOG.
SIGNAL MIRROR: REFLECTS THE SUN TO SIGNAL PASSING RESCUE PLANES.
BRAIDED CORD: FOR TYING STUFF TOGETHER.
NEEDLES AND THREAD: THREAD HOLDS 10 LBS AND CAN BE USED AS FISHING LINE.
MINI MEDICAL KIT: COLLECTION OF MEDICINES, INCLUDING PAIN RELIEVERS, ANTIBIOTICS AND WATER PURIFICATION TABLETS.
COMPASS: SO YOU ALWAYS KNOW WHICH WAY IS NORTH.
DUCT TAPE: PERFECT FOR REPAIRS OR ANYTHING ELSE YOU CAN THINK OF.
BAND-AIDS: FOR SIMPLE CUTS AND SCRAPES.
SCALPEL BLADE SEALED IN FOIL: FOR DELICATE MEDICAL CUTTING.
THERE'S MORE TO ME THAN YOU THINK, DEVIN. I WASN'T ALWAYS A PENCIL PUSHER, YOU KNOW.

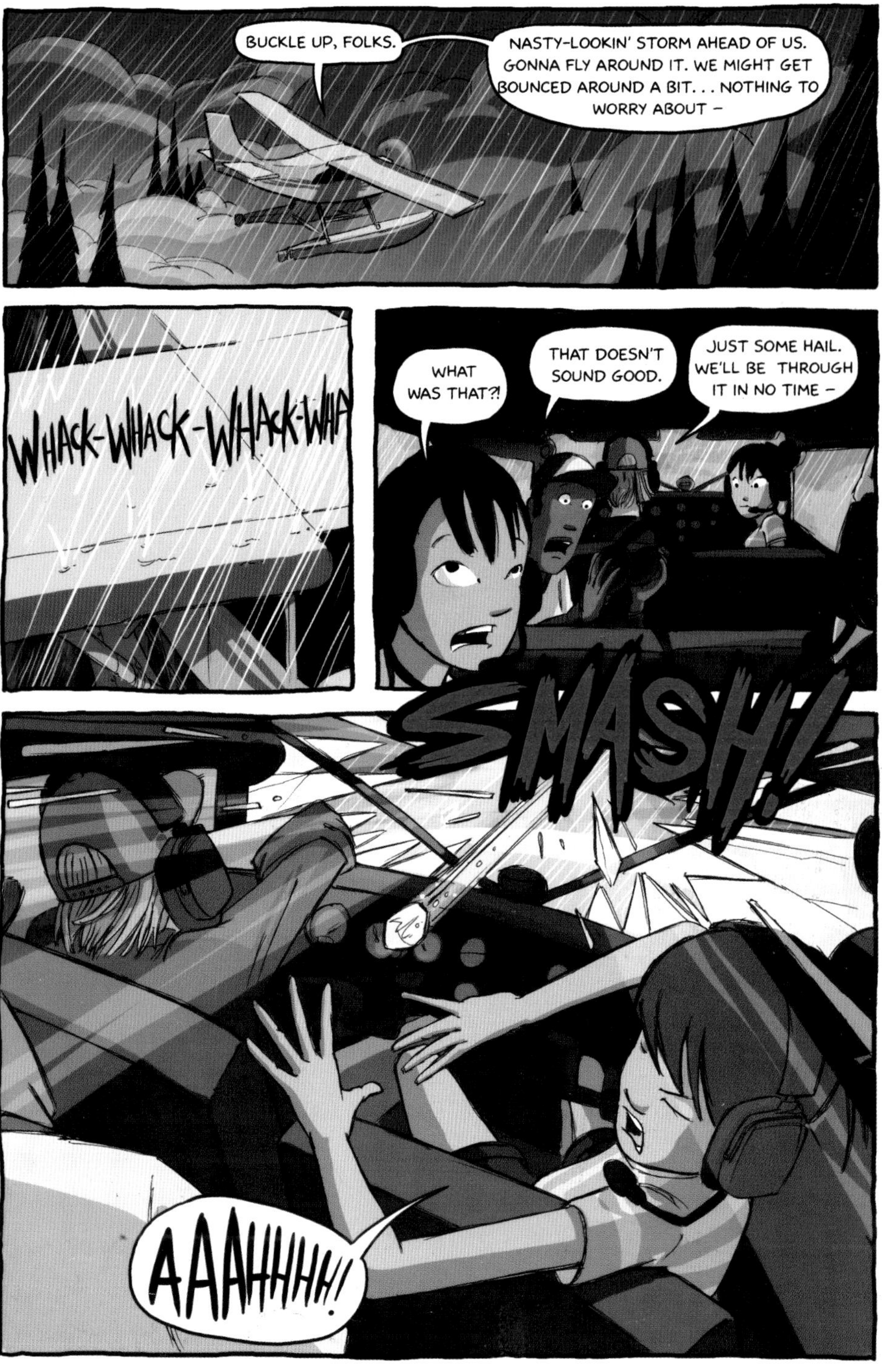

BUCKLE UP, FOLKS.
NASTY-LOOKIN' STORM AHEAD OF US. GONNA FLY AROUND IT. WE MIGHT GET BOUNCED AROUND A BIT. . . NOTHING TO WORRY ABOUT –
WHACK-WHACK-WHACK-WHA
WHAT WAS THAT?!
THAT DOESN'T SOUND GOOD.
JUST SOME HAIL. WE'LL BE THROUGH IT IN NO TIME –
SMASH!!
AAAHHHH!

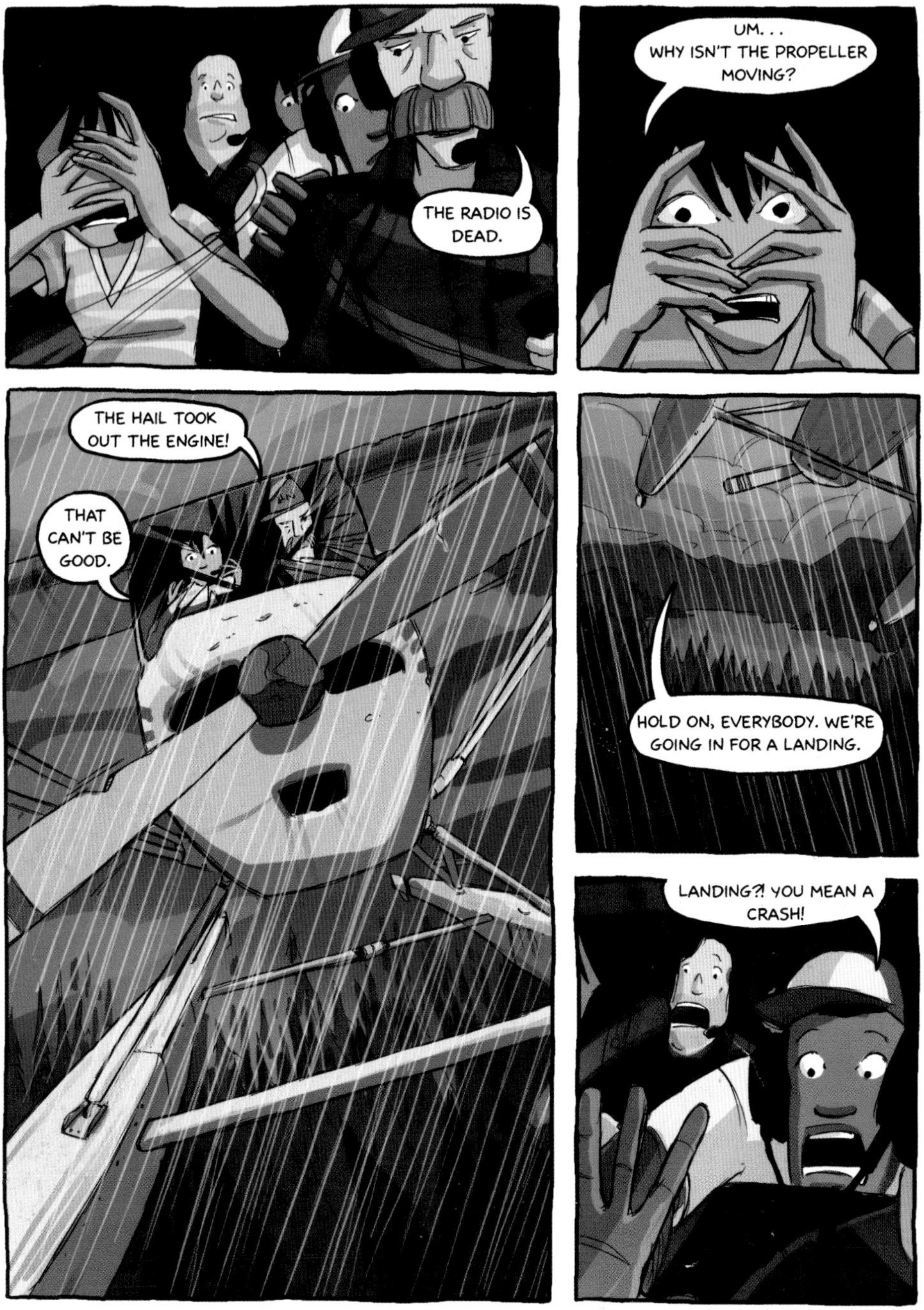
THE RADIO IS DEAD.
UM. . . WHY ISN'T THE PROPELLER MOVING?
THE HAIL TOOK OUT THE ENGINE!
THAT CAN'T BE GOOD.
HOLD ON, EVERYBODY. WE'RE GOING IN FOR A LANDING.
LANDING?! YOU MEAN A CRASH!

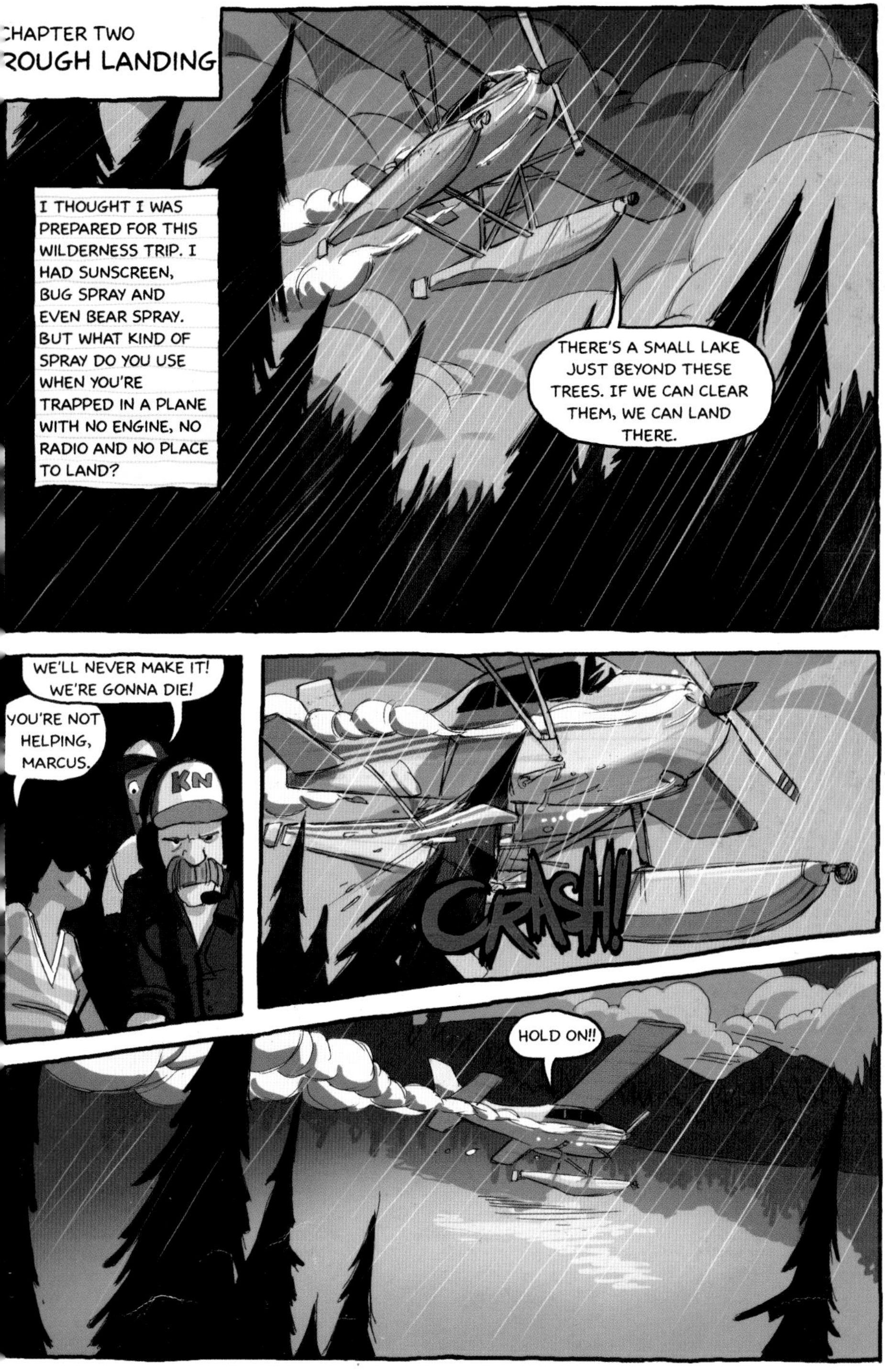
CHAPTER TWO
ROUGH LANDING
I THOUGHT I WAS PREPARED FOR THIS WILDERNESS TRIP. I HAD SUNSCREEN, BUG SPRAY AND EVEN BEAR SPRAY. BUT WHAT KIND OF SPRAY DO YOU USE WHEN YOU'RE TRAPPED IN A PLANE WITH NO ENGINE, NO RADIO AND NO PLACE TO LAND?
THERE'S A SMALL LAKE JUST BEYOND THESE TREES. IF WE CAN CLEAR THEM, WE CAN LAND THERE.
WE'LL NEVER MAKE IT! WE'RE GONNA DIE!
YOU'RE NOT HELPING, MARCUS.
KN
CRASH!
HOLD ON!!

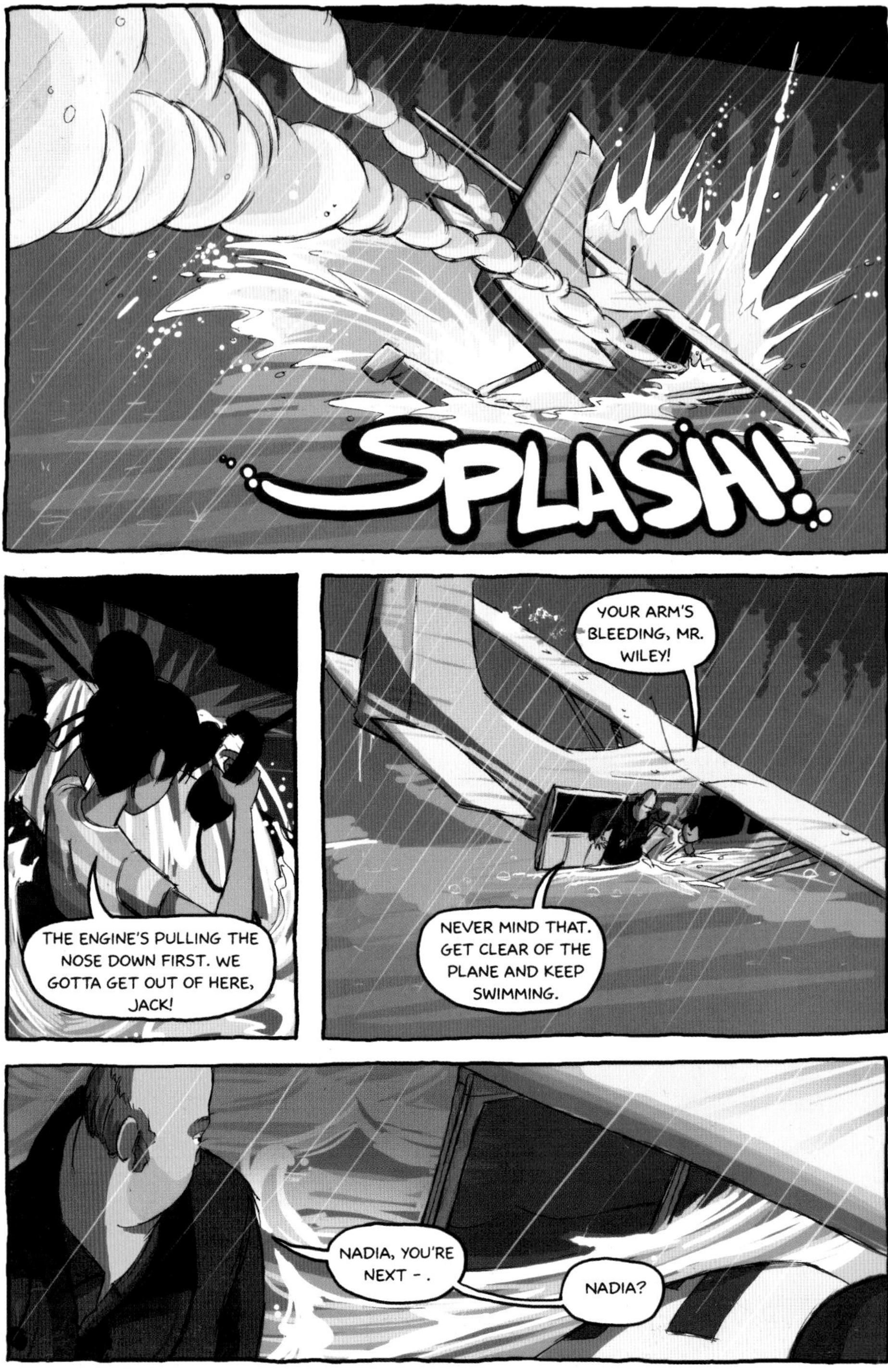
SPLASH!
THE ENGINE'S PULLING THE NOSE DOWN FIRST. WE GOTTA GET OUT OF HERE, JACK!
YOUR ARM'S BLEEDING, MR. WILEY!
NEVER MIND THAT. GET CLEAR OF THE PLANE AND KEEP SWIMMING.
NADIA, YOU'RE NEXT - .
NADIA?

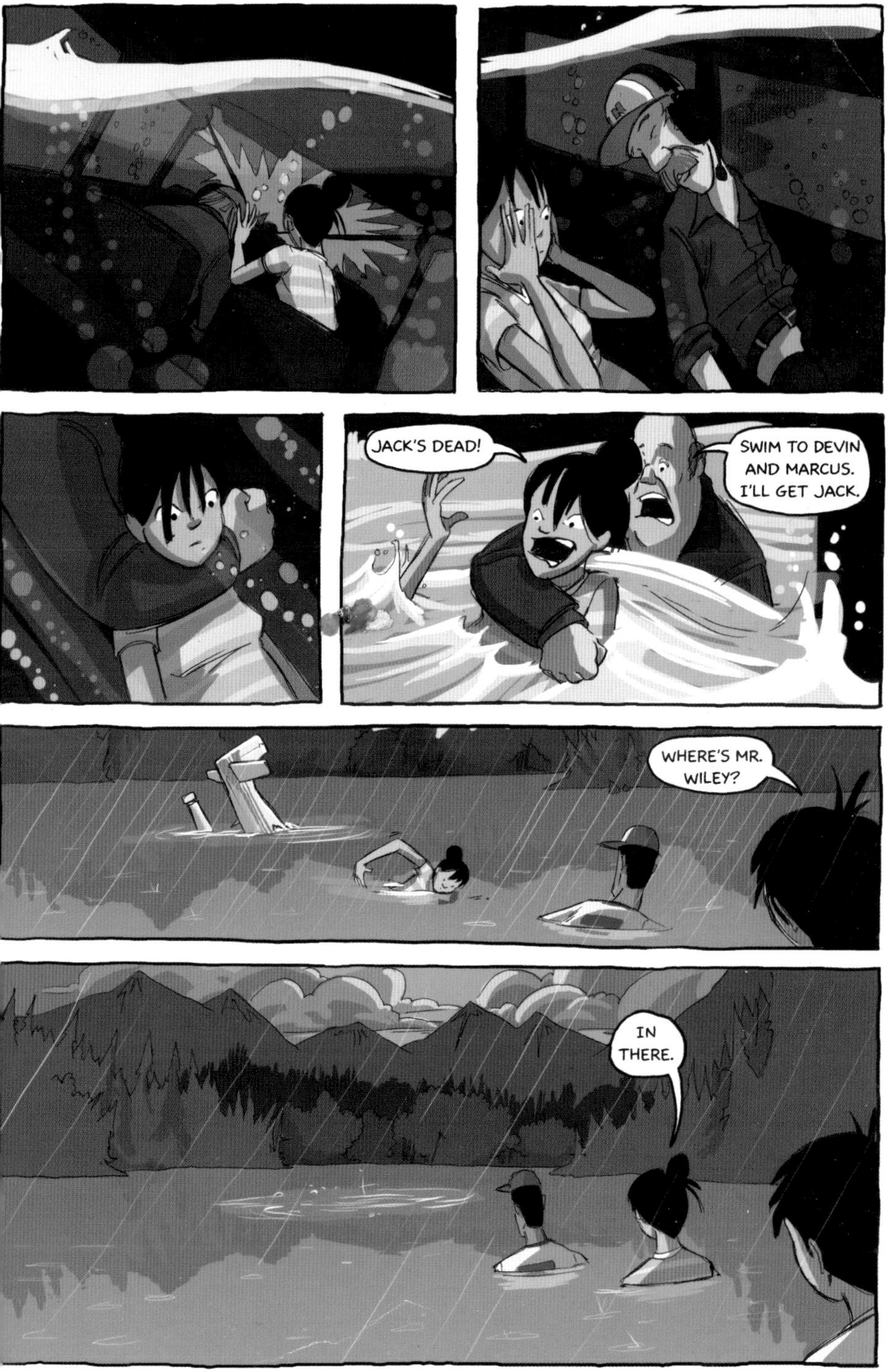
JACK'S DEAD!
SWIM TO DEVIN AND MARCUS. I'LL GET JACK.
WHERE'S MR. WILEY?
IN THERE.

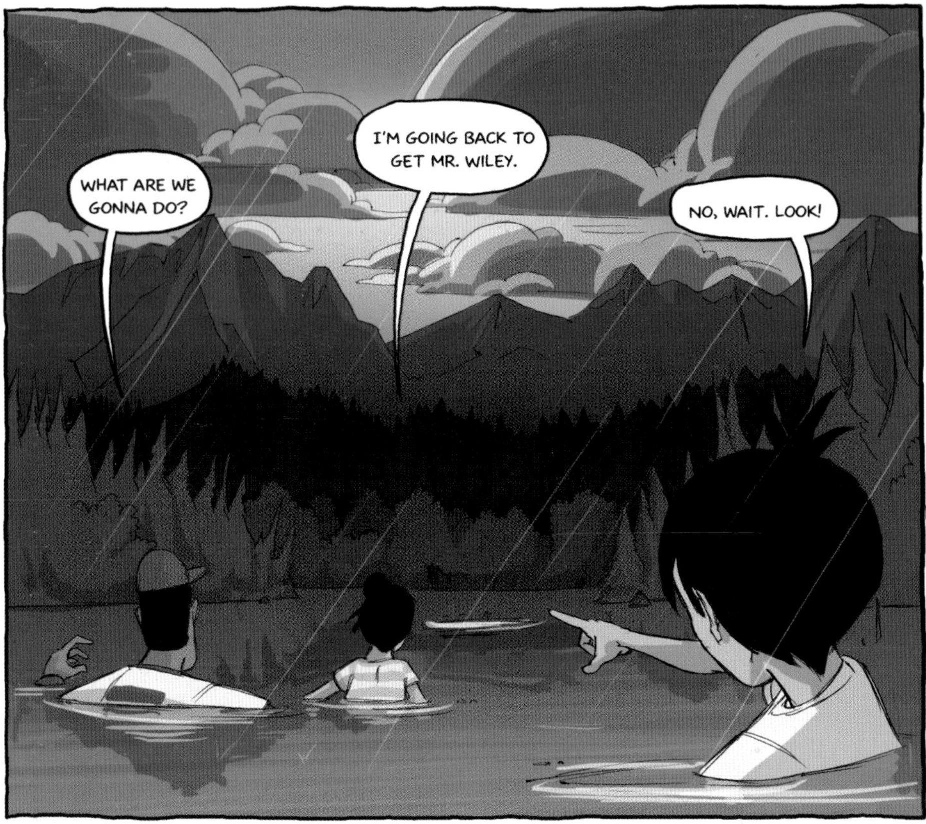
WHAT ARE WE GONNA DO?
I'M GOING BACK TO GET MR. WILEY.
NO, WAIT. LOOK!

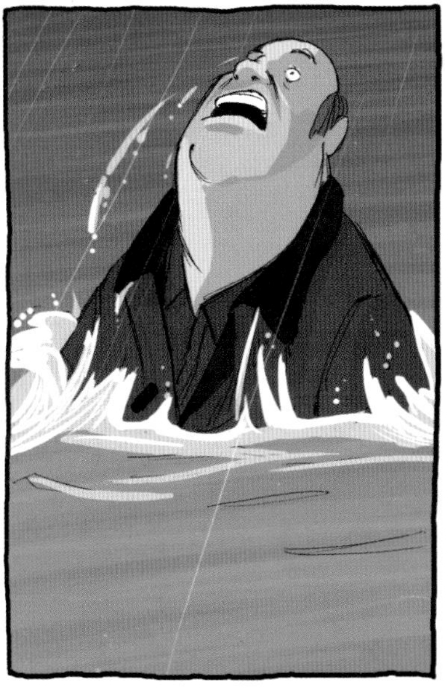

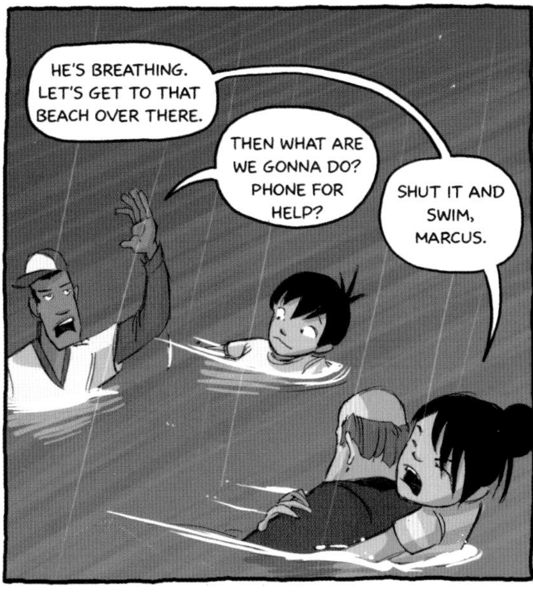
HE'S BREATHING. LET'S GET TO THAT BEACH OVER THERE.
THEN WHAT ARE WE GONNA DO? PHONE FOR HELP?
SHUT IT AND SWIM, MARCUS.

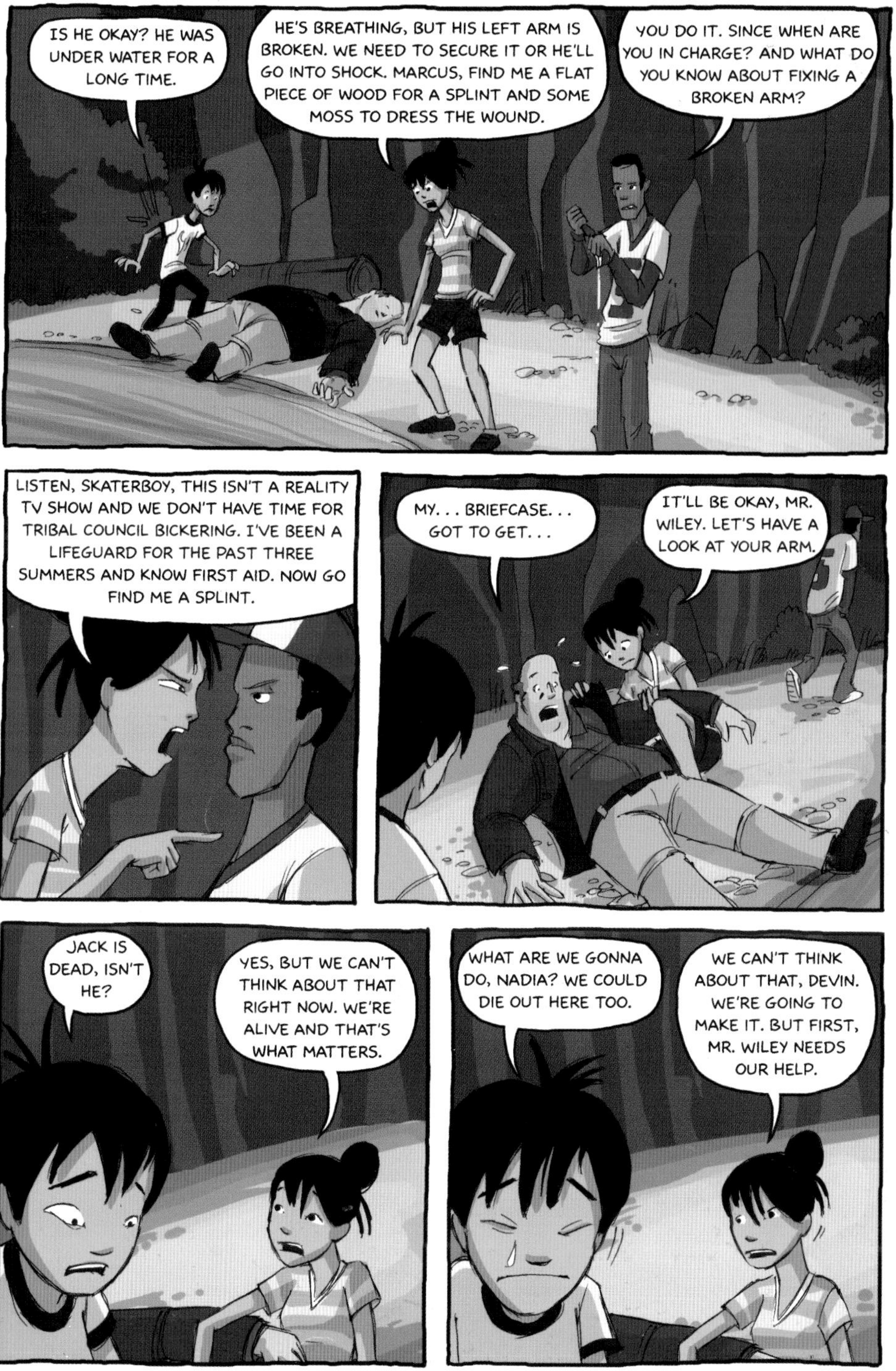
IS HE OKAY? HE WAS UNDER WATER FOR A LONG TIME.
HE'S BREATHING, BUT HIS LEFT ARM IS BROKEN. WE NEED TO SECURE IT OR HE'LL GO INTO SHOCK. MARCUS, FIND ME A FLAT PIECE OF WOOD FOR A SPLINT AND SOME MOSS TO DRESS THE WOUND.
YOU DO IT. SINCE WHEN ARE YOU IN CHARGE? AND WHAT DO YOU KNOW ABOUT FIXING A BROKEN ARM?
LISTEN, SKATERBOY, THIS ISN'T A REALITY TV SHOW AND WE DON'T HAVE TIME FOR TRIBAL COUNCIL BICKERING. I'VE BEEN A LIFEGUARD FOR THE PAST THREE SUMMERS AND KNOW FIRST AID. NOW GO FIND ME A SPLINT.
MY. . . BRIEFCASE. . . GOT TO GET. . .
IT'LL BE OKAY, MR. WILEY. LET'S HAVE A LOOK AT YOUR ARM.
JACK IS DEAD, ISN'T HE?
YES, BUT WE CAN'T THINK ABOUT THAT RIGHT NOW. WE'RE ALIVE AND THAT'S WHAT MATTERS.
WHAT ARE WE GONNA DO, NADIA? WE COULD DIE OUT HERE TOO.
WE CAN'T THINK ABOUT THAT, DEVIN. WE'RE GOING TO MAKE IT. BUT FIRST, MR. WILEY NEEDS OUR HELP.

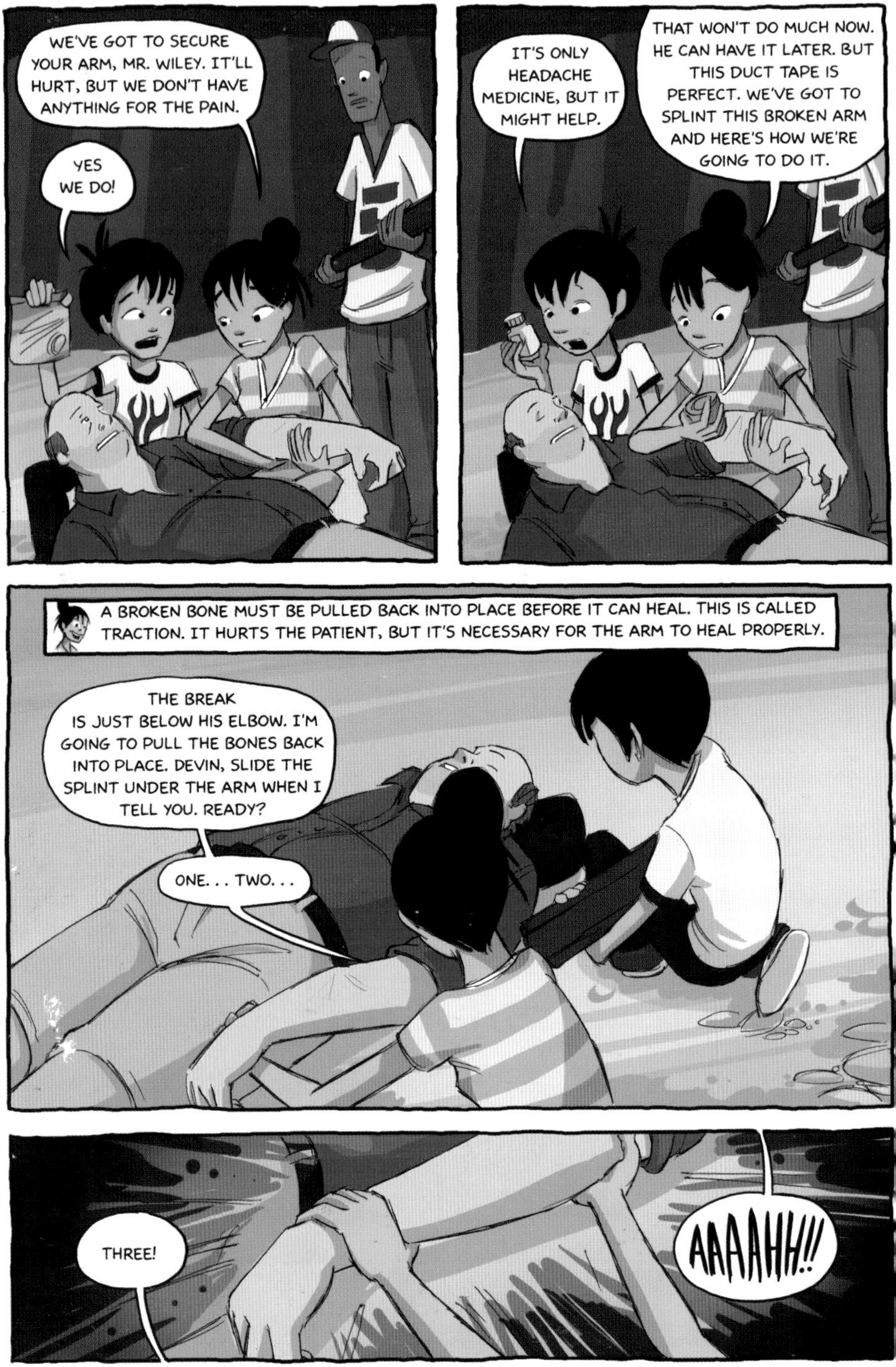
WE'VE GOT TO SECURE YOUR ARM, MR. WILEY. IT'LL HURT, BUT WE DON'T HAVE ANYTHING FOR THE PAIN.
YES WE DO!
IT'S ONLY HEADACHE MEDICINE, BUT IT MIGHT HELP.
THAT WON'T DO MUCH NOW. HE CAN HAVE IT LATER. BUT THIS DUCT TAPE IS PERFECT. WE'VE GOT TO SPLINT THIS BROKEN ARM AND HERE'S HOW WE'RE GOING TO DO IT.
A BROKEN BONE MUST BE PULLED BACK INTO PLACE BEFORE IT CAN HEAL. THIS IS CALLED TRACTION. IT HURTS THE PATIENT, BUT IT'S NECESSARY FOR THE ARM TO HEAL PROPERLY.
THE BREAK IS JUST BELOW HIS ELBOW. I'M GOING TO PULL THE BONES BACK INTO PLACE. DEVIN, SLIDE THE SPLINT UNDER THE ARM WHEN I TELL YOU. READY?
ONE. . . TWO. . .
THREE!
AAAAHH!!

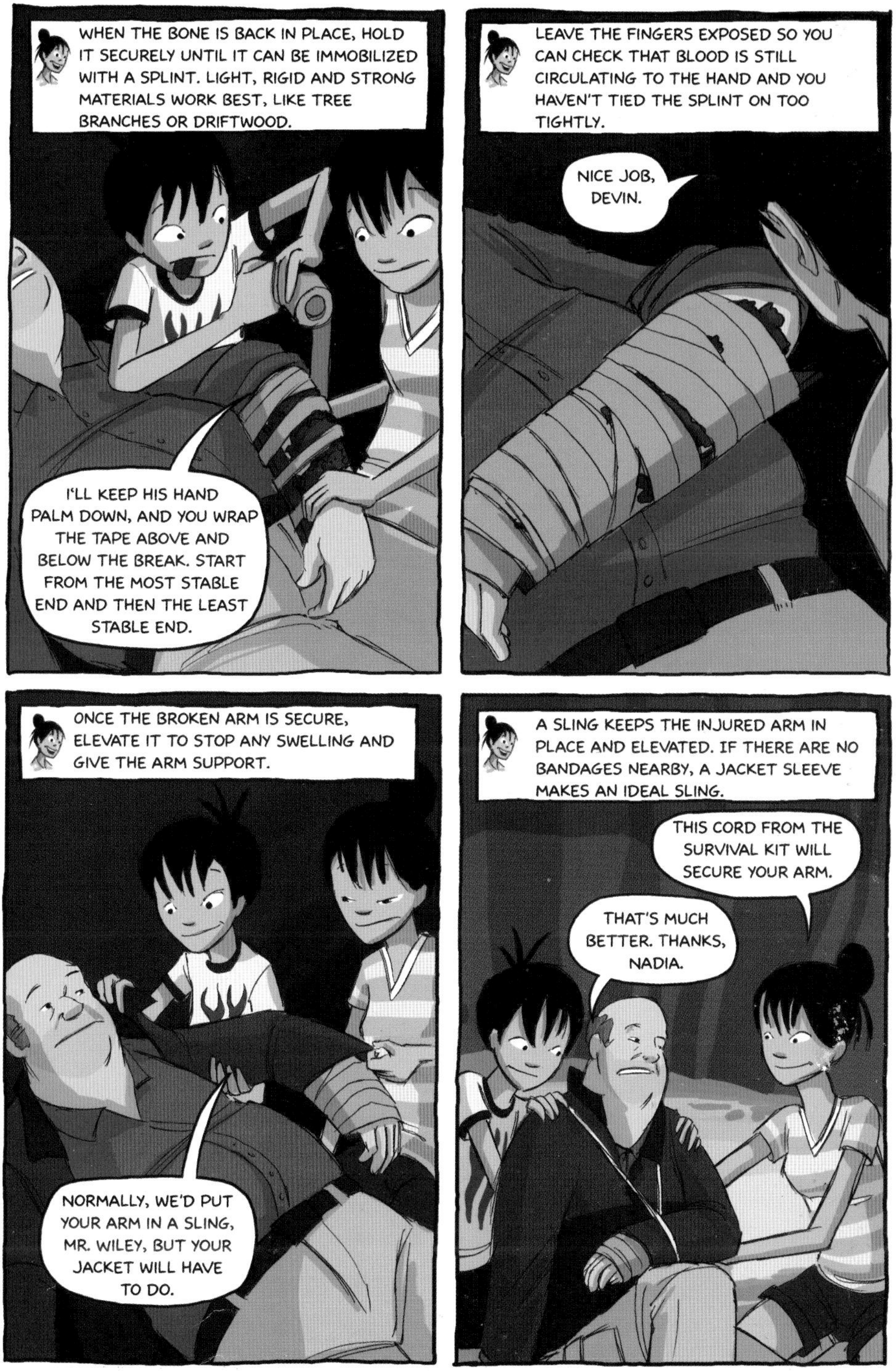

WHEN THE BONE IS BACK IN PLACE, HOLD IT SECURELY UNTIL IT CAN BE IMMOBILIZED WITH A SPLINT. LIGHT, RIGID AND STRONG MATERIALS WORK BEST, LIKE TREE BRANCHES OR DRIFTWOOD.
I'LL KEEP HIS HAND PALM DOWN, AND YOU WRAP THE TAPE ABOVE AND BELOW THE BREAK. START FROM THE MOST STABLE END AND THEN THE LEAST STABLE END.
LEAVE THE FINGERS EXPOSED SO YOU CAN CHECK THAT BLOOD IS STILL CIRCULATING TO THE HAND AND YOU HAVEN'T TIED THE SPLINT ON TOO TIGHTLY.
NICE JOB, DEVIN.
ONCE THE BROKEN ARM IS SECURE, ELEVATE IT TO STOP ANY SWELLING AND GIVE THE ARM SUPPORT.
NORMALLY, WE'D PUT YOUR ARM IN A SLING, MR. WILEY, BUT YOUR JACKET WILL HAVE TO DO.
A SLING KEEPS THE INJURED ARM IN PLACE AND ELEVATED. IF THERE ARE NO BANDAGES NEARBY, A JACKET SLEEVE MAKES AN IDEAL SLING.
THIS CORD FROM THE SURVIVAL KIT WILL SECURE YOUR ARM.
THAT'S MUCH BETTER. THANKS, NADIA.

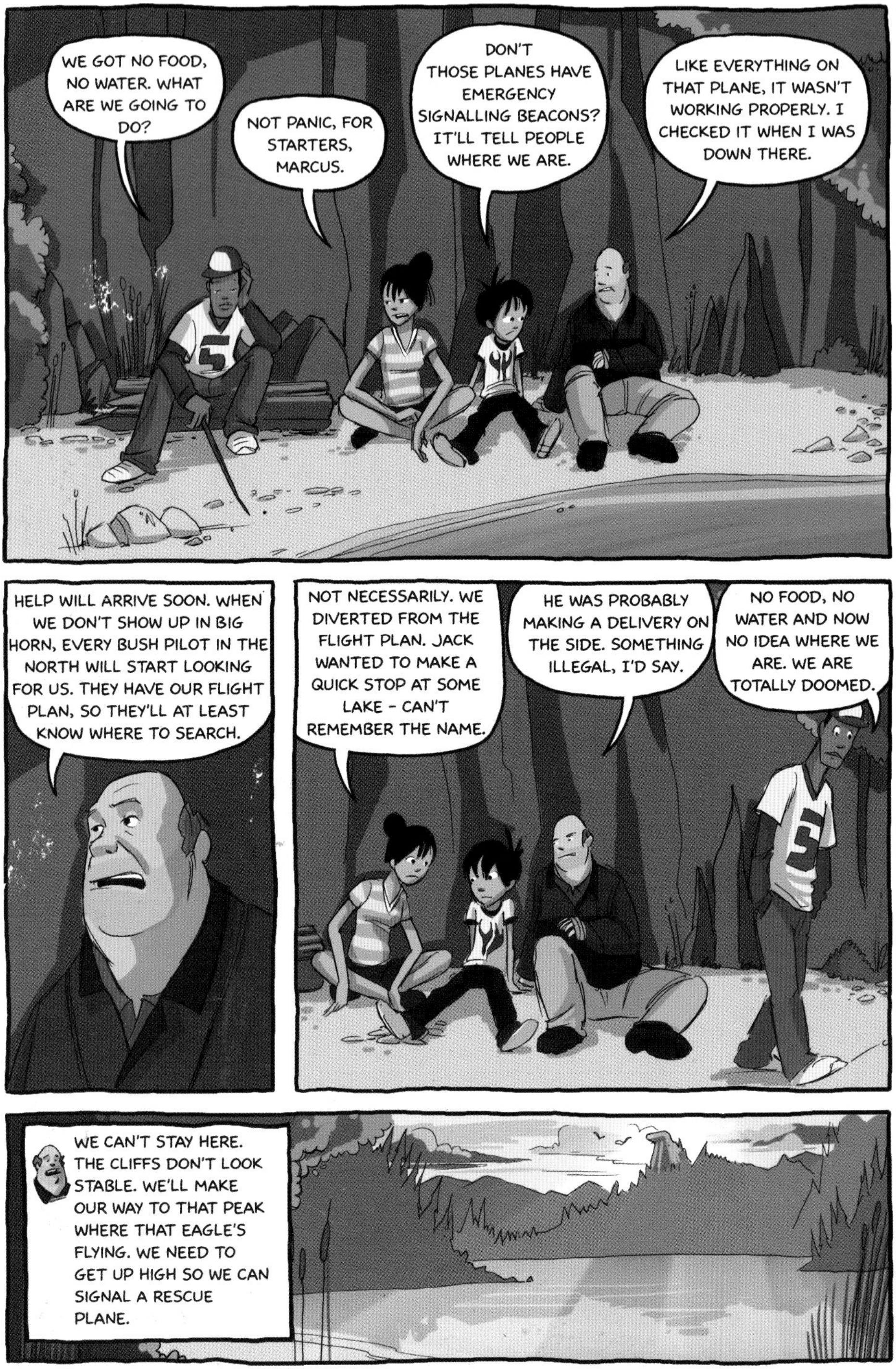
WE GOT NO FOOD, NO WATER. WHAT ARE WE GOING TO DO?
NOT PANIC, FOR STARTERS, MARCUS.
DON'T THOSE PLANES HAVE EMERGENCY SIGNALLING BEACONS? IT'LL TELL PEOPLE WHERE WE ARE.
LIKE EVERYTHING ON THAT PLANE, IT WASN'T WORKING PROPERLY. I CHECKED IT WHEN I WAS DOWN THERE.
HELP WILL ARRIVE SOON. WHEN WE DON'T SHOW UP IN BIG HORN, EVERY BUSH PILOT IN THE NORTH WILL START LOOKING FOR US. THEY HAVE OUR FLIGHT PLAN, SO THEY'LL AT LEAST KNOW WHERE TO SEARCH.
NOT NECESSARILY. WE DIVERTED FROM THE FLIGHT PLAN. JACK WANTED TO MAKE A QUICK STOP AT SOME LAKE - CAN'T REMEMBER THE NAME.
HE WAS PROBABLY MAKING A DELIVERY ON THE SIDE. SOMETHING ILLEGAL, I'D SAY.
NO FOOD, NO WATER AND NOW NO IDEA WHERE WE ARE. WE ARE TOTALLY DOOMED.
WE CAN'T STAY HERE. THE CLIFFS DON'T LOOK STABLE. WE'LL MAKE OUR WAY TO THAT PEAK WHERE THAT EAGLE'S FLYING. WE NEED TO GET UP HIGH SO WE CAN SIGNAL A RESCUE PLANE.

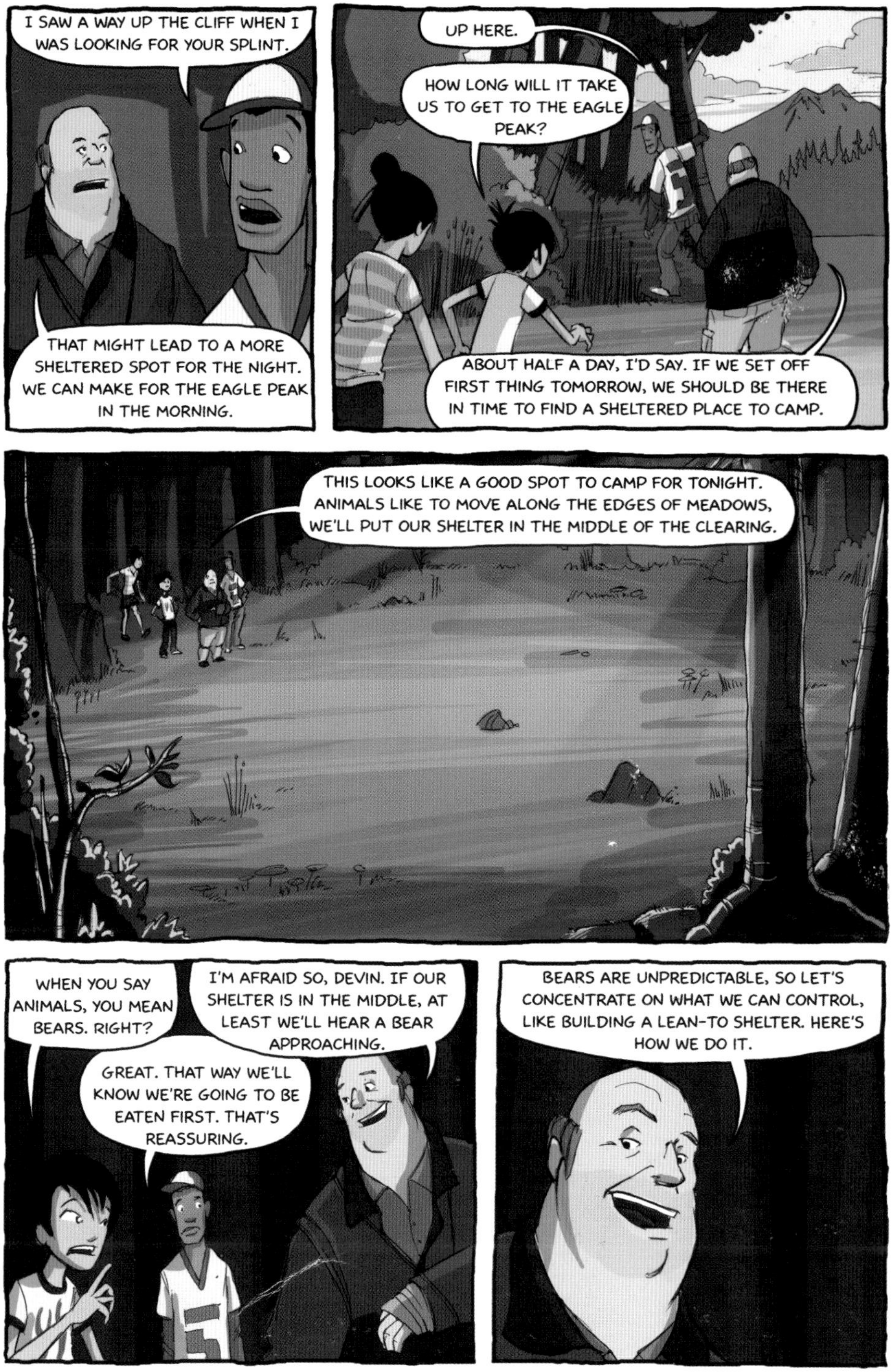
I SAW A WAY UP THE CLIFF WHEN I WAS LOOKING FOR YOUR SPLINT.
THAT MIGHT LEAD TO A MORE SHELTERED SPOT FOR THE NIGHT. WE CAN MAKE FOR THE EAGLE PEAK IN THE MORNING.
UP HERE.
HOW LONG WILL IT TAKE US TO GET TO THE EAGLE PEAK?
ABOUT HALF A DAY, I'D SAY. IF WE SET OFF FIRST THING TOMORROW, WE SHOULD BE THERE IN TIME TO FIND A SHELTERED PLACE TO CAMP.
THIS LOOKS LIKE A GOOD SPOT TO CAMP FOR TONIGHT. ANIMALS LIKE TO MOVE ALONG THE EDGES OF MEADOWS, WE'LL PUT OUR SHELTER IN THE MIDDLE OF THE CLEARING.
WHEN YOU SAY ANIMALS, YOU MEAN BEARS. RIGHT?
I'M AFRAID SO, DEVIN. IF OUR SHELTER IS IN THE MIDDLE, AT LEAST WE'LL HEAR A BEAR APPROACHING.
GREAT. THAT WAY WE'LL KNOW WE'RE GOING TO BE EATEN FIRST. THAT'S REASSURING.
BEARS ARE UNPREDICTABLE, SO LET'S CONCENTRATE ON WHAT WE CAN CONTROL, LIKE BUILDING A LEAN-TO SHELTER. HERE'S HOW WE DO IT.

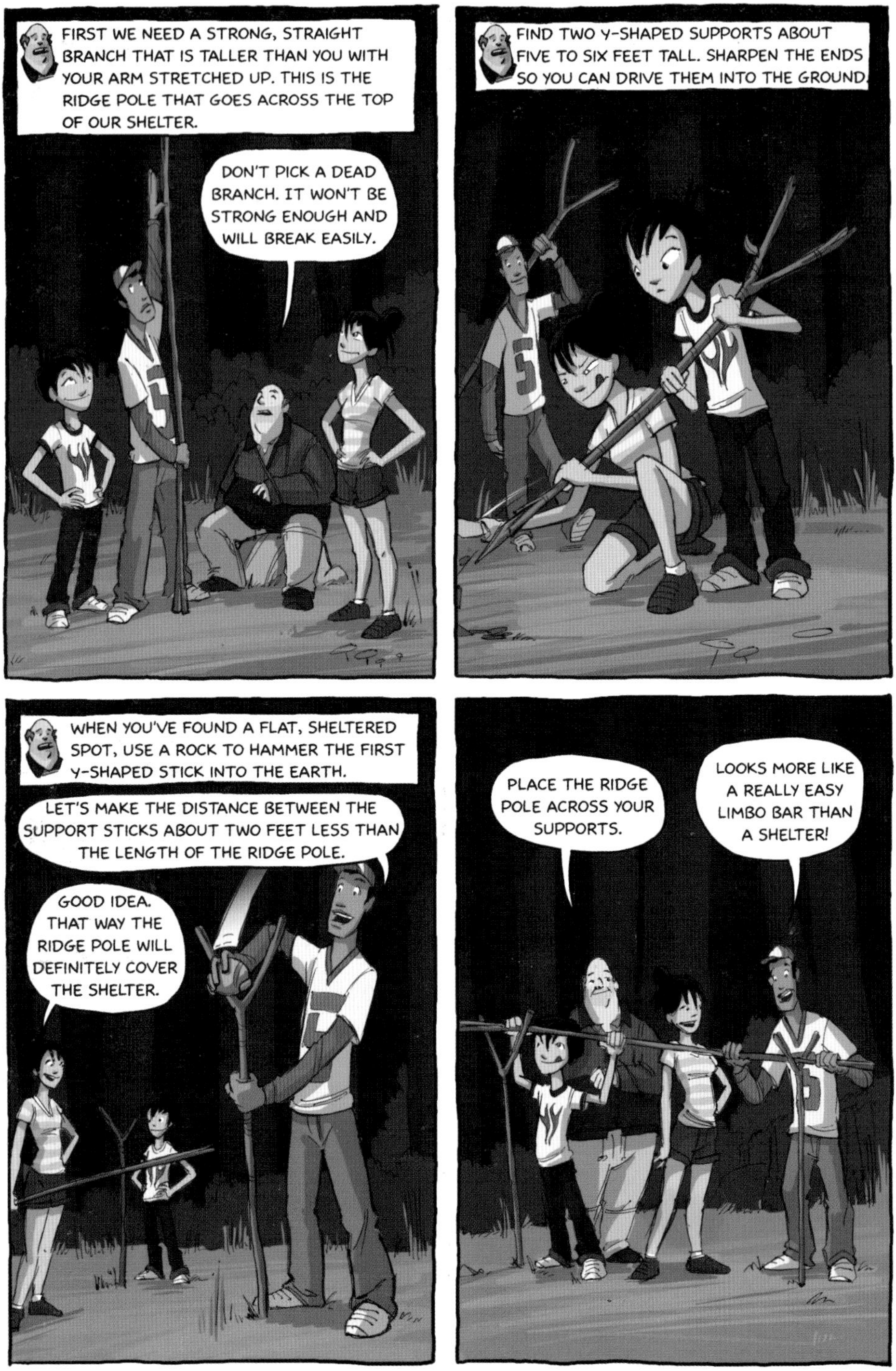
FIRST WE NEED A STRONG, STRAIGHT BRANCH THAT IS TALLER THAN YOU WITH YOUR ARM STRETCHED UP. THIS IS THE RIDGE POLE THAT GOES ACROSS THE TOP OF OUR SHELTER.
DON'T PICK A DEAD BRANCH. IT WON'T BE STRONG ENOUGH AND WILL BREAK EASILY.
FIND TWO Y-SHAPED SUPPORTS ABOUT FIVE TO SIX FEET TALL. SHARPEN THE ENDS SO YOU CAN DRIVE THEM INTO THE GROUND.
WHEN YOU'VE FOUND A FLAT, SHELTERED SPOT, USE A ROCK TO HAMMER THE FIRST Y-SHAPED STICK INTO THE EARTH.
LET'S MAKE THE DISTANCE BETWEEN THE SUPPORT STICKS ABOUT TWO FEET LESS THAN THE LENGTH OF THE RIDGE POLE.
GOOD IDEA. THAT WAY THE RIDGE POLE WILL DEFINITELY COVER THE SHELTER.
PLACE THE RIDGE POLE ACROSS YOUR SUPPORTS.
LOOKS MORE LIKE A REALLY EASY LIMBO BAR THAN A SHELTER!

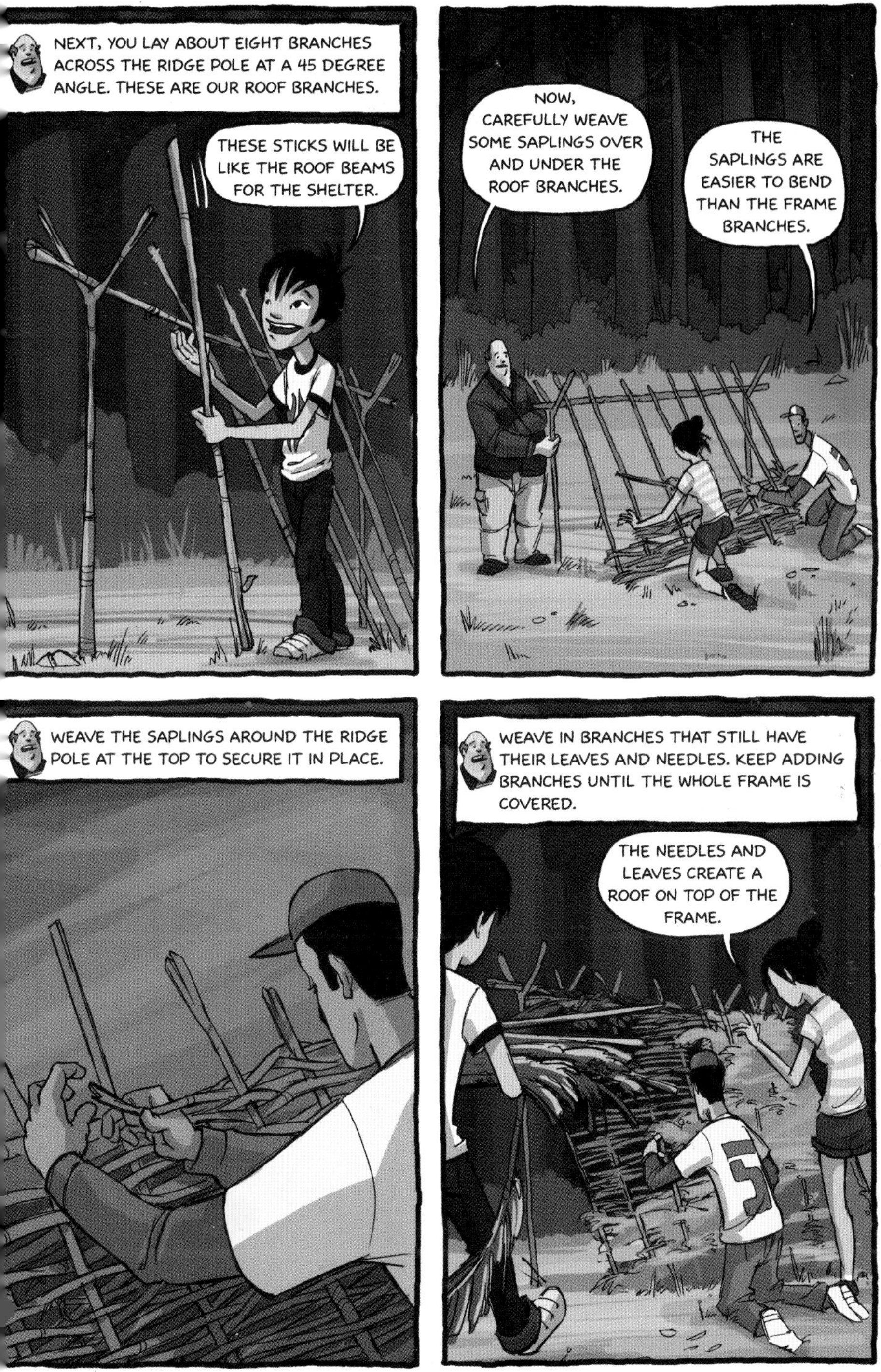
NEXT, YOU LAY ABOUT EIGHT BRANCHES ACROSS THE RIDGE POLE AT A 45 DEGREE ANGLE. THESE ARE OUR ROOF BRANCHES.
THESE STICKS WILL BE LIKE THE ROOF BEAMS FOR THE SHELTER.
NOW, CAREFULLY WEAVE SOME SAPLINGS OVER AND UNDER THE ROOF BRANCHES.
THE SAPLINGS ARE EASIER TO BEND THAN THE FRAME BRANCHES.
WEAVE THE SAPLINGS AROUND THE RIDGE POLE AT THE TOP TO SECURE IT IN PLACE.
WEAVE IN BRANCHES THAT STILL HAVE THEIR LEAVES AND NEEDLES. KEEP ADDING BRANCHES UNTIL THE WHOLE FRAME IS COVERED.
THE NEEDLES AND LEAVES CREATE A ROOF ON TOP OF THE FRAME.

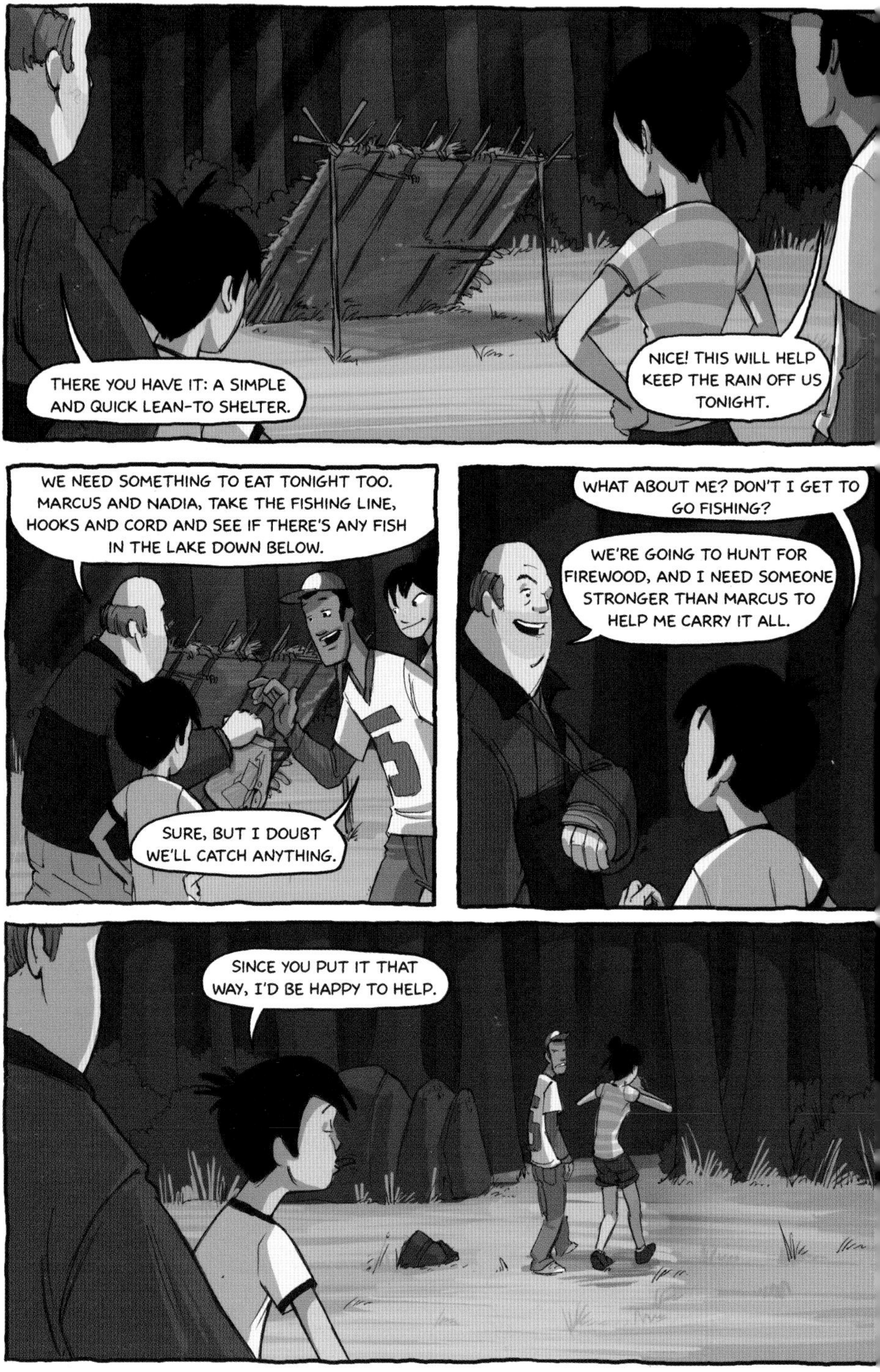
THERE YOU HAVE IT: A SIMPLE AND QUICK LEAN-TO SHELTER.
NICE! THIS WILL HELP KEEP THE RAIN OFF US TONIGHT.
WE NEED SOMETHING TO EAT TONIGHT TOO. MARCUS AND NADIA, TAKE THE FISHING LINE, HOOKS AND CORD AND SEE IF THERE'S ANY FISH IN THE LAKE DOWN BELOW.
SURE, BUT I DOUBT WE'LL CATCH ANYTHING.
WHAT ABOUT ME? DON'T I GET TO GO FISHING?
WE'RE GOING TO HUNT FOR FIREWOOD, AND I NEED SOMEONE STRONGER THAN MARCUS TO HELP ME CARRY IT ALL.
SINCE YOU PUT IT THAT WAY, I'D BE HAPPY TO HELP.

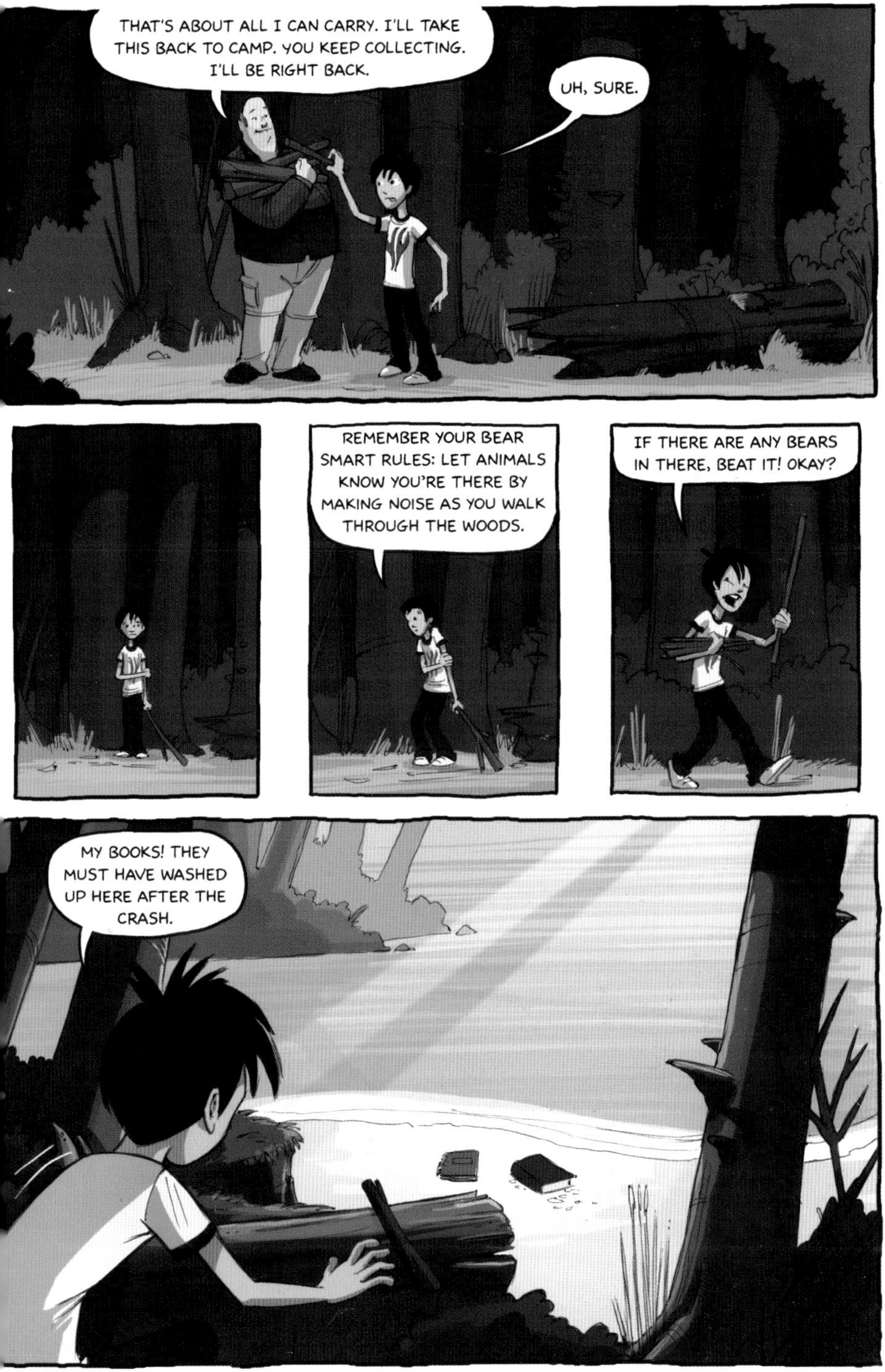
THAT'S ABOUT ALL I CAN CARRY. I'LL TAKE THIS BACK TO CAMP. YOU KEEP COLLECTING. I'LL BE RIGHT BACK.
UH, SURE.
REMEMBER YOUR BEAR SMART RULES: LET ANIMALS KNOW YOU'RE THERE BY MAKING NOISE AS YOU WALK THROUGH THE WOODS.
IF THERE ARE ANY BEARS IN THERE, BEAT IT! OKAY?
MY BOOKS! THEY MUST HAVE WASHED UP HERE AFTER THE CRASH.

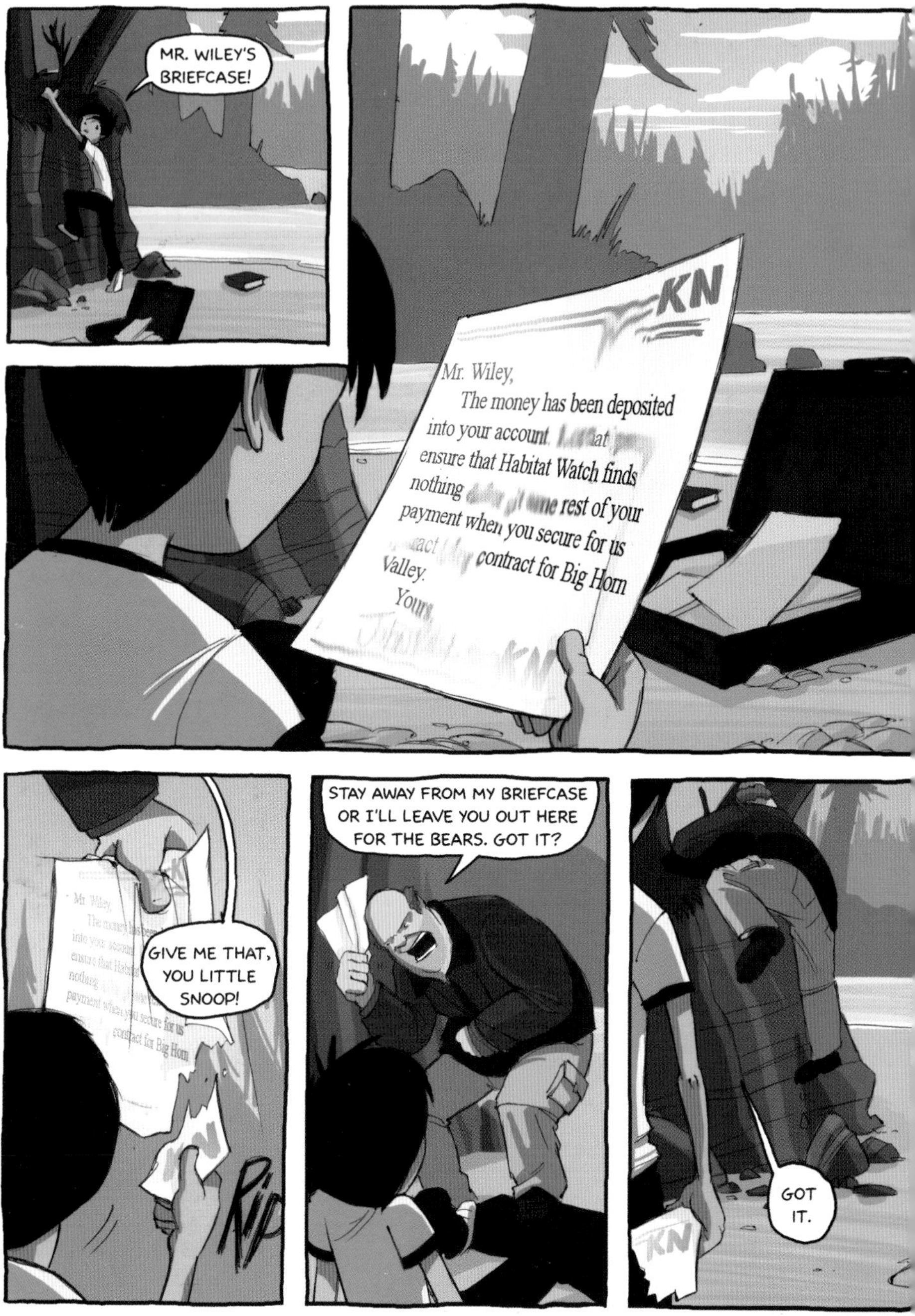
MR. WILEY'S BRIEFCASE!
KN
Mr. Wiley,
The money has been deposited
into your account
ensure that Habitat Watch finds
nothing
rest of your
payment when you secure for us
contract for Big Horn
Valley.
Yours,
GIVE ME THAT, YOU LITTLE SNOOP!
STAY AWAY FROM MY BRIEFCASE OR I'LL LEAVE YOU OUT HERE FOR THE BEARS. GOT IT?
GOT IT.
KN

HAPTER THREE

'ALLEY OF 'ECRETS

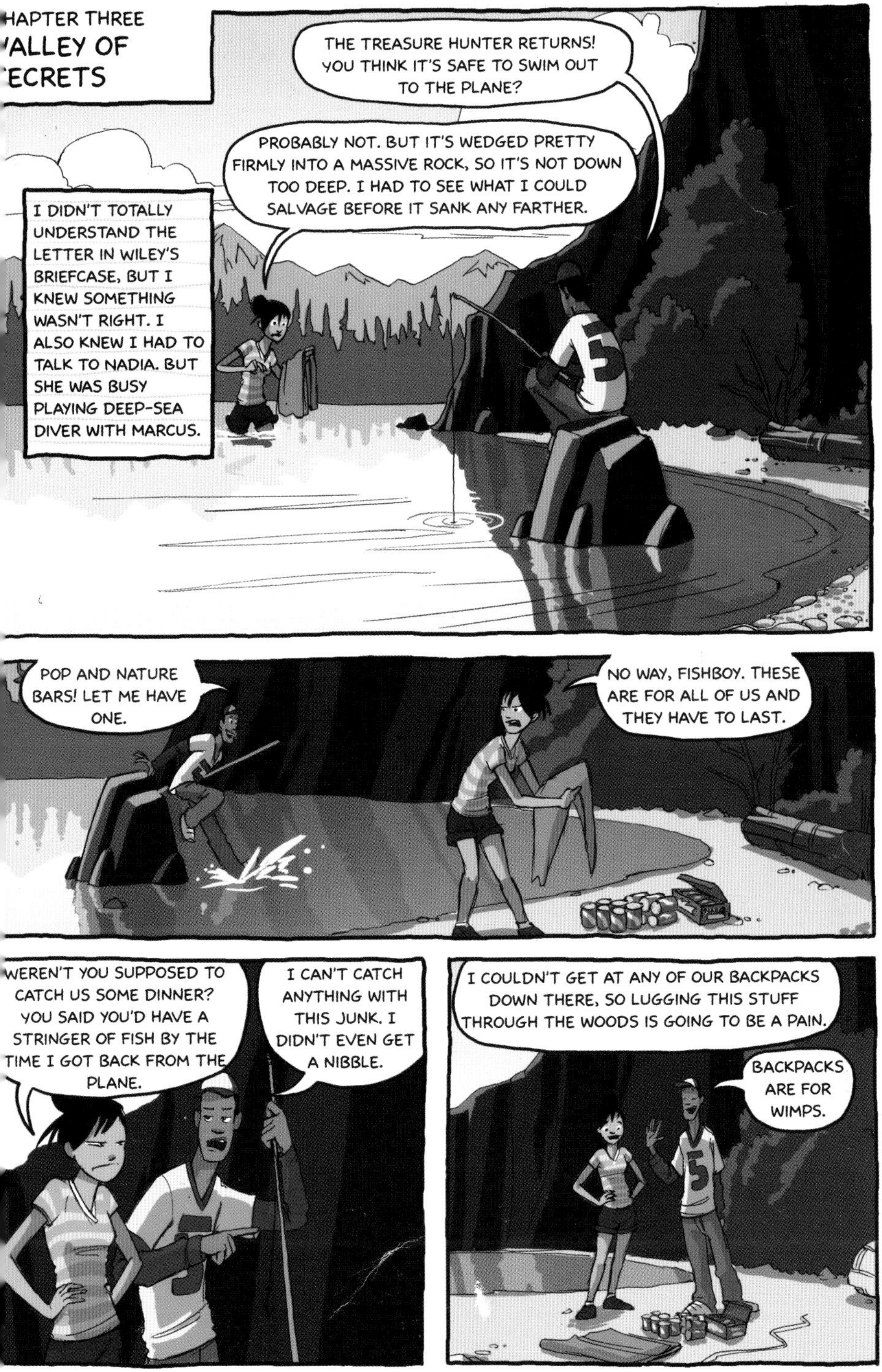
THE TREASURE HUNTER RETURNS! YOU THINK IT'S SAFE TO SWIM OUT TO THE PLANE?
PROBABLY NOT. BUT IT'S WEDGED PRETTY FIRMLY INTO A MASSIVE ROCK, SO IT'S NOT DOWN TOO DEEP. I HAD TO SEE WHAT I COULD SALVAGE BEFORE IT SANK ANY FARTHER.
I DIDN'T TOTALLY UNDERSTAND THE LETTER IN WILEY'S BRIEFCASE, BUT I KNEW SOMETHING WASN'T RIGHT. I ALSO KNEW I HAD TO TALK TO NADIA. BUT SHE WAS BUSY PLAYING DEEP-SEA DIVER WITH MARCUS.
POP AND NATURE BARS! LET ME HAVE ONE.
NO WAY, FISHBOY. THESE ARE FOR ALL OF US AND THEY HAVE TO LAST.
WEREN'T YOU SUPPOSED TO CATCH US SOME DINNER? YOU SAID YOU'D HAVE A STRINGER OF FISH BY THE TIME I GOT BACK FROM THE PLANE.
I CAN'T CATCH ANYTHING WITH THIS JUNK. I DIDN'T EVEN GET A NIBBLE.
I COULDN'T GET AT ANY OF OUR BACKPACKS DOWN THERE, SO LUGGING THIS STUFF THROUGH THE WOODS IS GOING TO BE A PAIN.
BACKPACKS ARE FOR WIMPS.

WE'LL CARRY THE GEAR OLD SCHOOL, LIKE THE EARLY EXPLORERS DID – IN A HUDSON'S BAY PACK. I'LL SHOW YOU HOW TO MAKE ONE.

THIS PACK CAN BE MADE WITH ANY STURDY MATERIAL, LIKE A GROUNDSHEET OR A BLANKET LIKE THIS ONE.

FIRST, FOLD THE BLANKET UNTIL IT'S ABOUT 1 METER SQUARE.

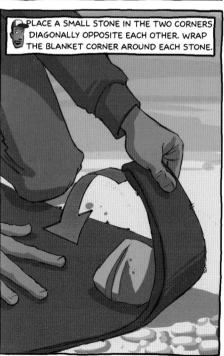

PLACE A SMALL STONE IN THE TWO CORNERS DIAGONALLY OPPOSITE EACH OTHER. WRAP THE BLANKET CORNER AROUND EACH STONE.

TIE THE BLANKET UNDER THE STONE WITH A SHORT PIECE OF CORD. THIS WILL HOLD IT IN PLACE AND CREATE A SECURE TYING POINT ON THE BLANKET.

GOOD THING WE HAD THAT CORD IN WILEY'S SURVIVAL KIT.

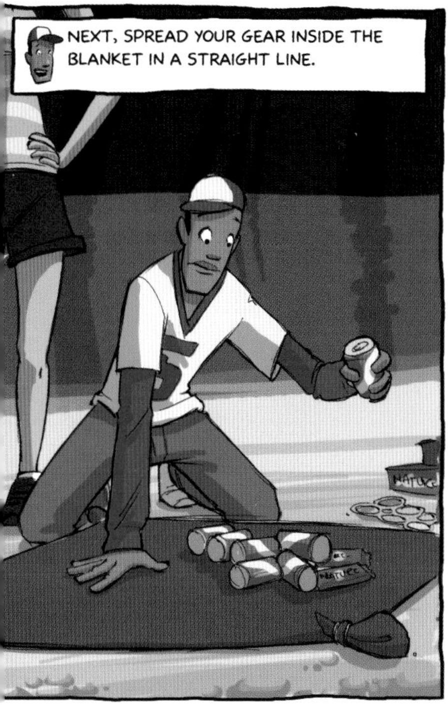
NEXT, SPREAD YOUR GEAR INSIDE THE BLANKET IN A STRAIGHT LINE.
NATURE
NATURE
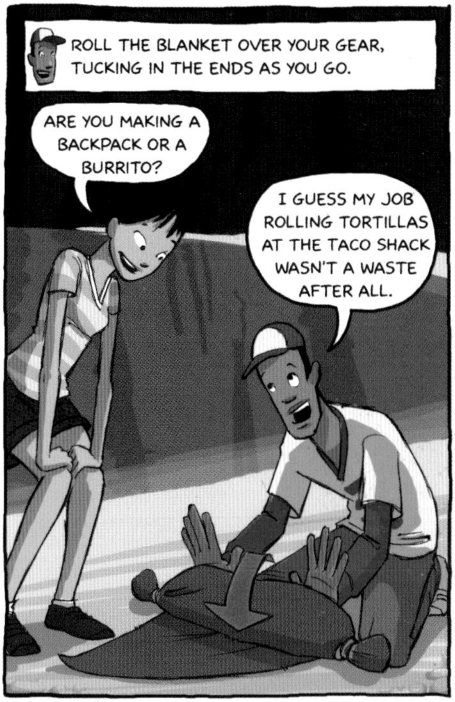
ROLL THE BLANKET OVER YOUR GEAR, TUCKING IN THE ENDS AS YOU GO.
ARE YOU MAKING A BACKPACK OR A BURRITO?
I GUESS MY JOB ROLLING TORTILLAS AT THE TACO SHACK WASN'T A WASTE AFTER ALL.
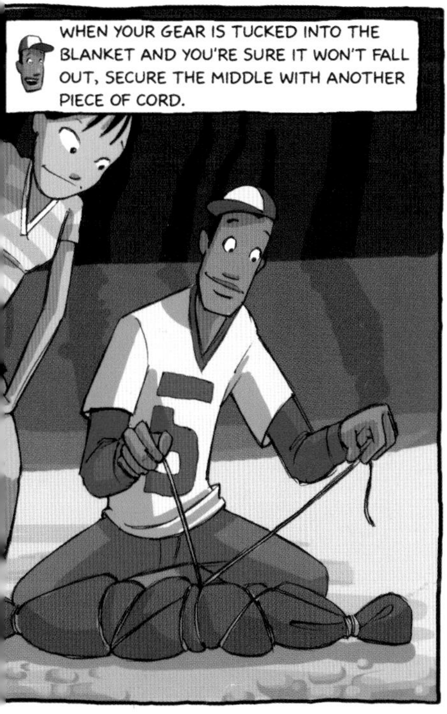
WHEN YOUR GEAR IS TUCKED INTO THE BLANKET AND YOU'RE SURE IT WON'T FALL OUT, SECURE THE MIDDLE WITH ANOTHER PIECE OF CORD.
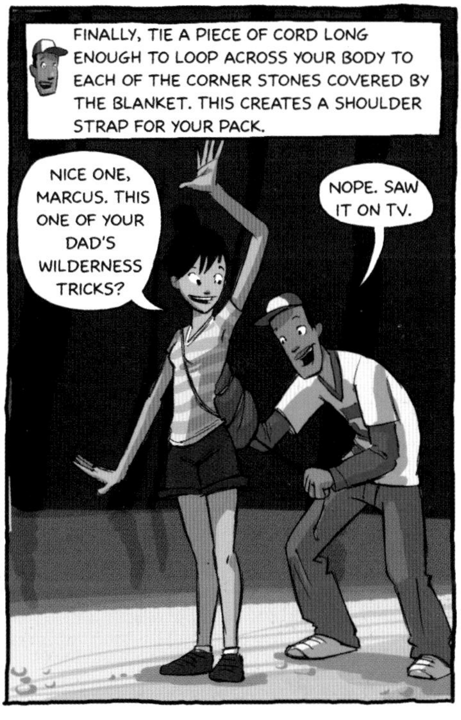
FINALLY, TIE A PIECE OF CORD LONG ENOUGH TO LOOP ACROSS YOUR BODY TO EACH OF THE CORNER STONES COVERED BY THE BLANKET. THIS CREATES A SHOULDER STRAP FOR YOUR PACK.
NICE ONE, MARCUS. THIS ONE OF YOUR DAD'S WILDERNESS TRICKS?
NOPE. SAW IT ON TV.

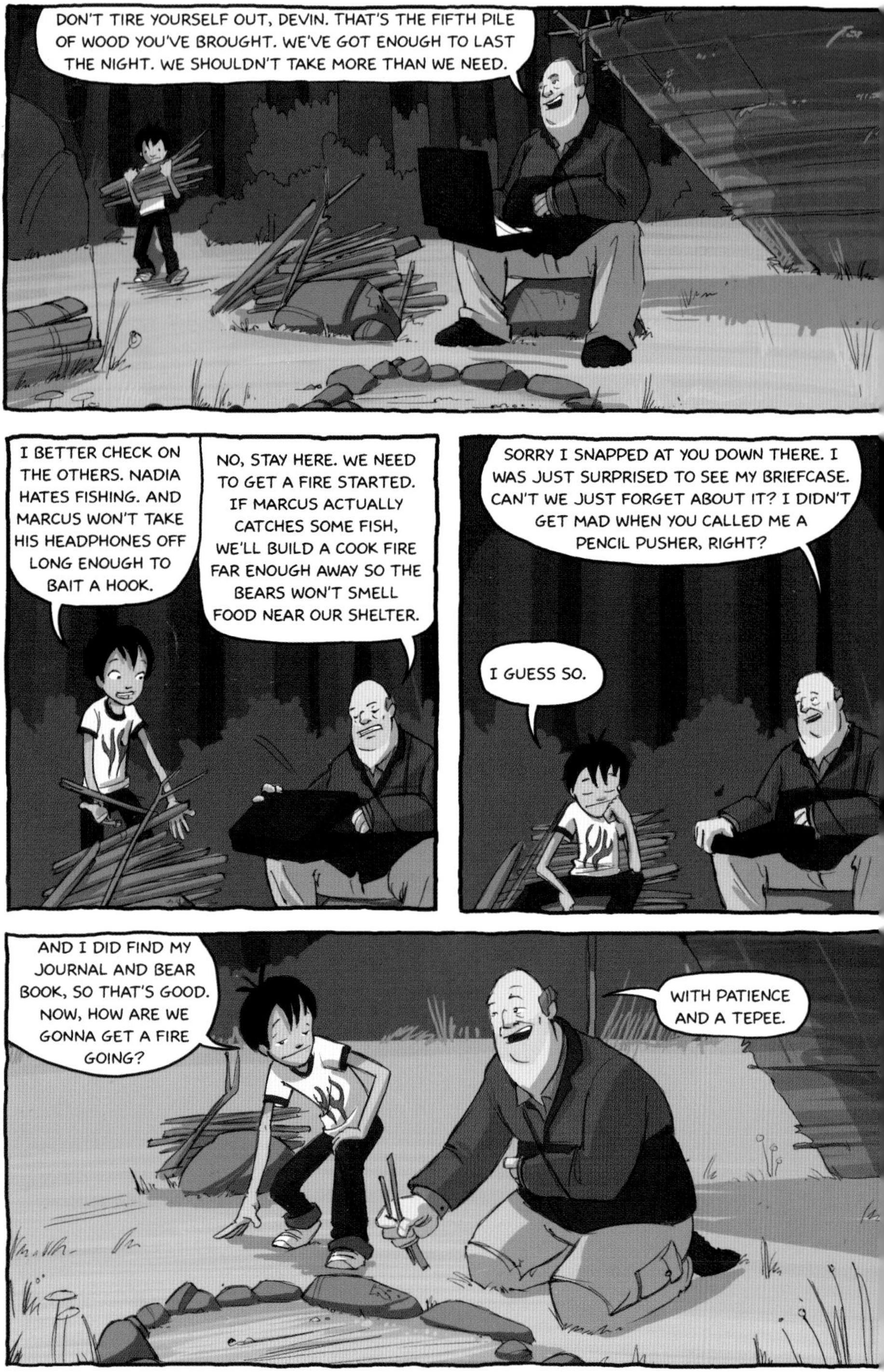
DON'T TIRE YOURSELF OUT, DEVIN. THAT'S THE FIFTH PILE OF WOOD YOU'VE BROUGHT. WE'VE GOT ENOUGH TO LAST THE NIGHT. WE SHOULDN'T TAKE MORE THAN WE NEED.
I BETTER CHECK ON THE OTHERS. NADIA HATES FISHING. AND MARCUS WON'T TAKE HIS HEADPHONES OFF LONG ENOUGH TO BAIT A HOOK.
NO, STAY HERE. WE NEED TO GET A FIRE STARTED. IF MARCUS ACTUALLY CATCHES SOME FISH, WE'LL BUILD A COOK FIRE FAR ENOUGH AWAY SO THE BEARS WON'T SMELL FOOD NEAR OUR SHELTER.
SORRY I SNAPPED AT YOU DOWN THERE. I WAS JUST SURPRISED TO SEE MY BRIEFCASE. CAN'T WE JUST FORGET ABOUT IT? I DIDN'T GET MAD WHEN YOU CALLED ME A PENCIL PUSHER, RIGHT?
I GUESS SO.
AND I DID FIND MY JOURNAL AND BEAR BOOK, SO THAT'S GOOD. NOW, HOW ARE WE GONNA GET A FIRE GOING?
WITH PATIENCE AND A TEPEE.

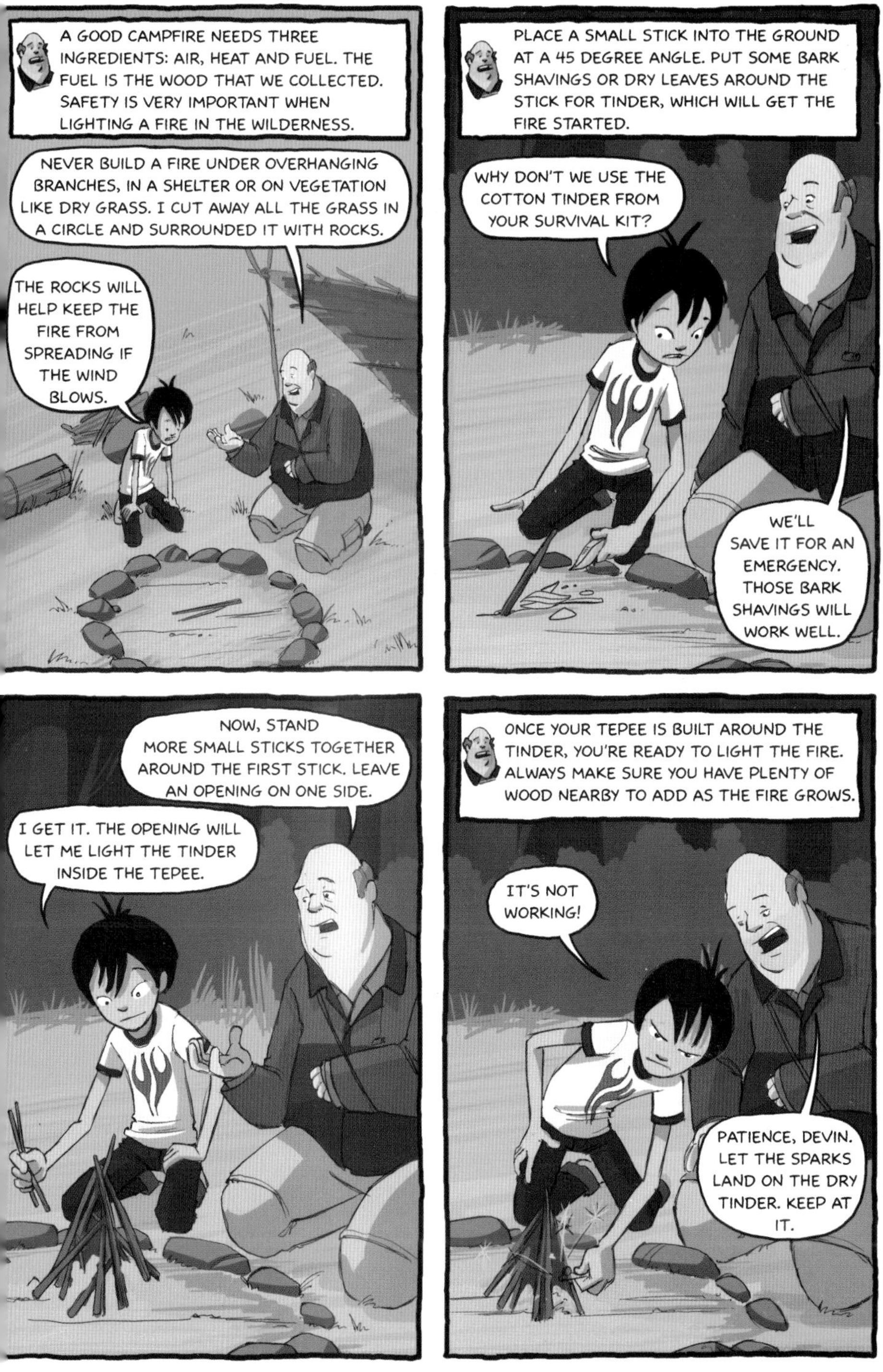

A GOOD CAMPFIRE NEEDS THREE INGREDIENTS: AIR, HEAT AND FUEL. THE FUEL IS THE WOOD THAT WE COLLECTED. SAFETY IS VERY IMPORTANT WHEN LIGHTING A FIRE IN THE WILDERNESS.
NEVER BUILD A FIRE UNDER OVERHANGING BRANCHES, IN A SHELTER OR ON VEGETATION LIKE DRY GRASS. I CUT AWAY ALL THE GRASS IN A CIRCLE AND SURROUNDED IT WITH ROCKS.
THE ROCKS WILL HELP KEEP THE FIRE FROM SPREADING IF THE WIND BLOWS.
PLACE A SMALL STICK INTO THE GROUND AT A 45 DEGREE ANGLE. PUT SOME BARK SHAVINGS OR DRY LEAVES AROUND THE STICK FOR TINDER, WHICH WILL GET THE FIRE STARTED.
WHY DON'T WE USE THE COTTON TINDER FROM YOUR SURVIVAL KIT?
WE'LL SAVE IT FOR AN EMERGENCY. THOSE BARK SHAVINGS WILL WORK WELL.
NOW, STAND MORE SMALL STICKS TOGETHER AROUND THE FIRST STICK. LEAVE AN OPENING ON ONE SIDE.
I GET IT. THE OPENING WILL LET ME LIGHT THE TINDER INSIDE THE TEPEE.
ONCE YOUR TEPEE IS BUILT AROUND THE TINDER, YOU'RE READY TO LIGHT THE FIRE. ALWAYS MAKE SURE YOU HAVE PLENTY OF WOOD NEARBY TO ADD AS THE FIRE GROWS.
IT'S NOT WORKING!
PATIENCE, DEVIN. LET THE SPARKS LAND ON THE DRY TINDER. KEEP AT IT.

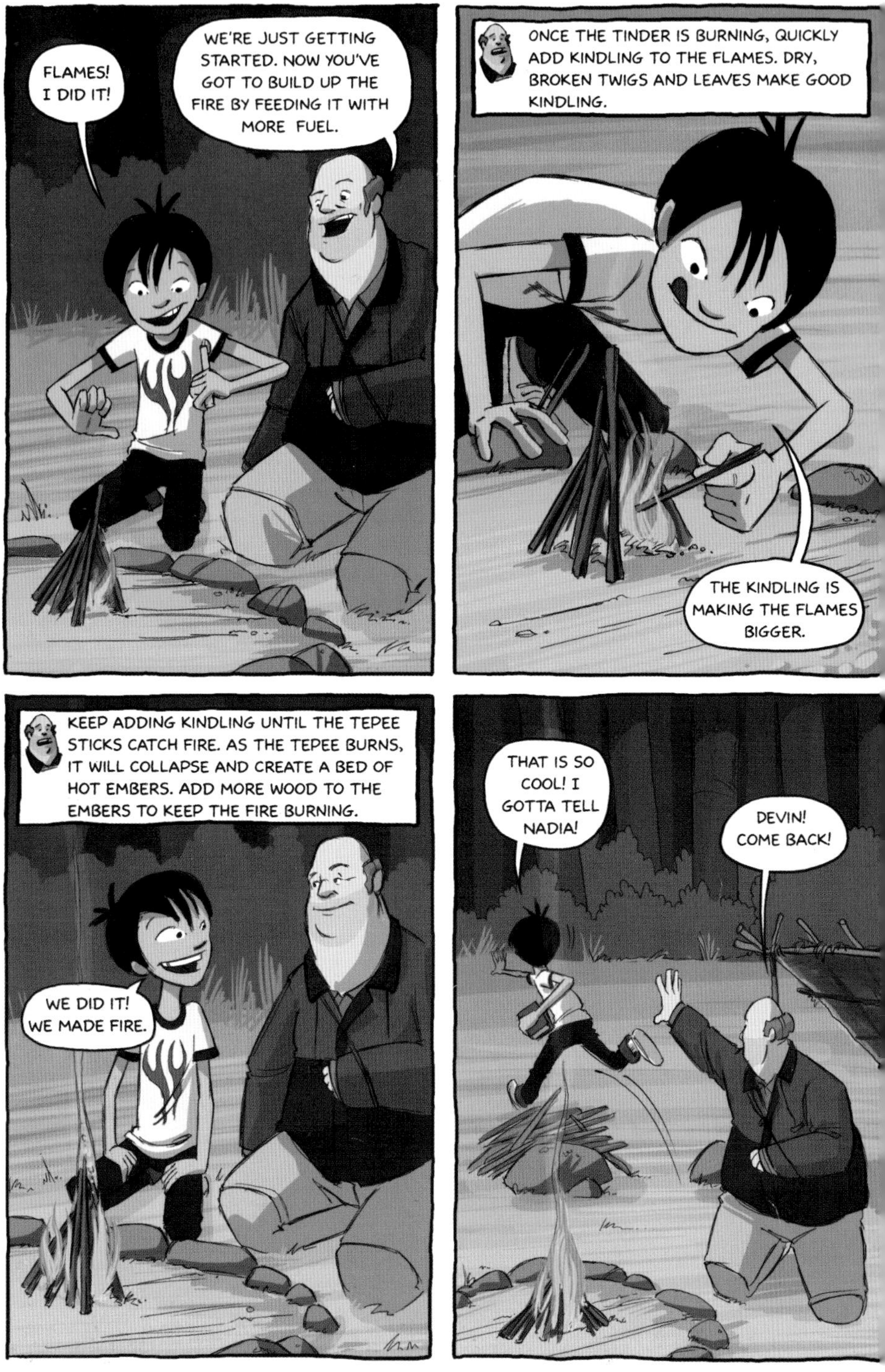
FLAMES! I DID IT!
WE'RE JUST GETTING STARTED. NOW YOU'VE GOT TO BUILD UP THE FIRE BY FEEDING IT WITH MORE FUEL.
ONCE THE TINDER IS BURNING, QUICKLY ADD KINDLING TO THE FLAMES. DRY, BROKEN TWIGS AND LEAVES MAKE GOOD KINDLING.
THE KINDLING IS MAKING THE FLAMES BIGGER.
KEEP ADDING KINDLING UNTIL THE TEPEE STICKS CATCH FIRE. AS THE TEPEE BURNS, IT WILL COLLAPSE AND CREATE A BED OF HOT EMBERS. ADD MORE WOOD TO THE EMBERS TO KEEP THE FIRE BURNING.
WE DID IT! WE MADE FIRE.
THAT IS SO COOL! I GOTTA TELL NADIA!
DEVIN! COME BACK!

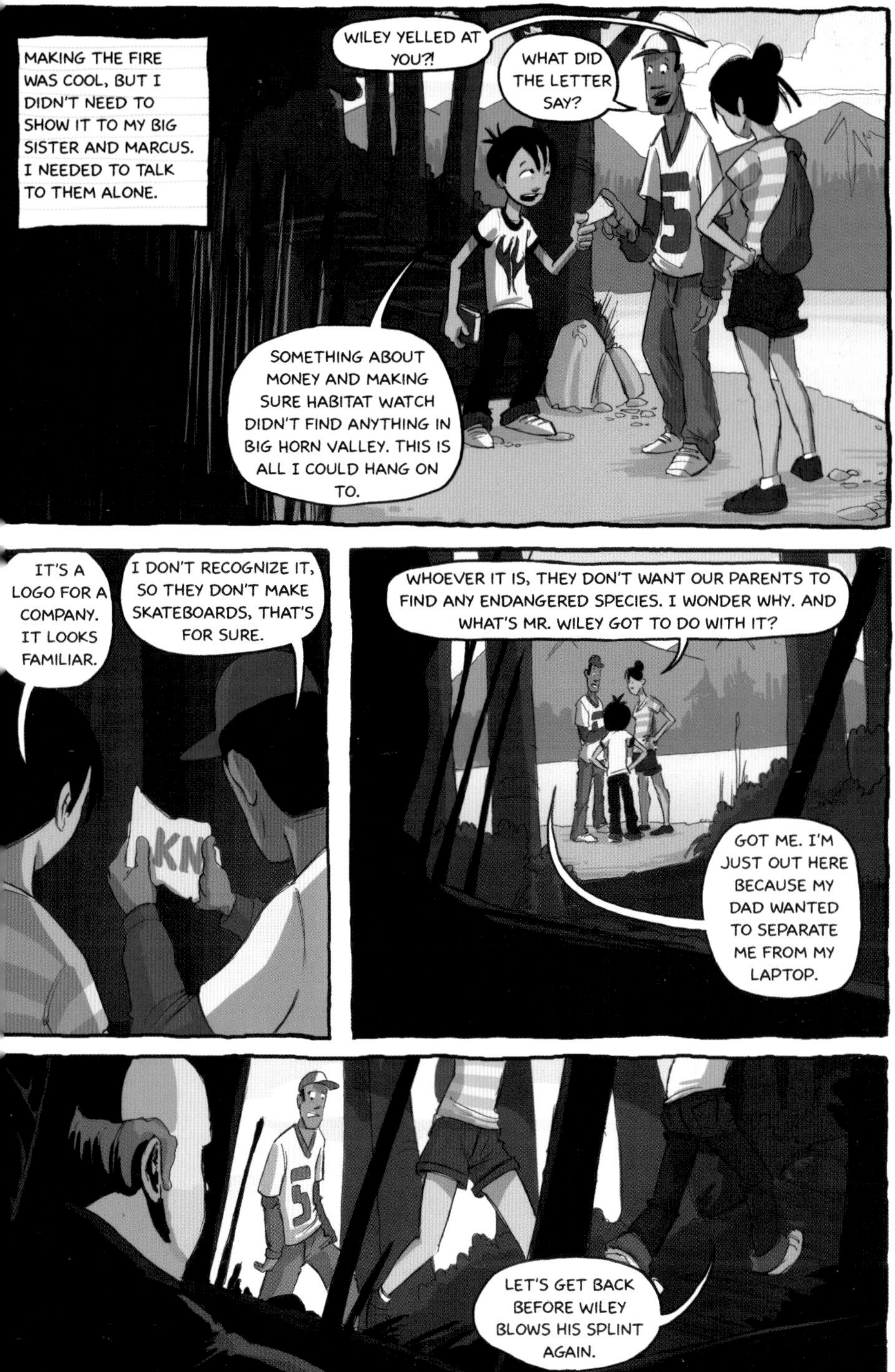
MAKING THE FIRE WAS COOL, BUT I DIDN'T NEED TO SHOW IT TO MY BIG SISTER AND MARCUS. I NEEDED TO TALK TO THEM ALONE.
WILEY YELLED AT YOU?!
WHAT DID THE LETTER SAY?
SOMETHING ABOUT MONEY AND MAKING SURE HABITAT WATCH DIDN'T FIND ANYTHING IN BIG HORN VALLEY. THIS IS ALL I COULD HANG ON TO.
IT'S A LOGO FOR A COMPANY. IT LOOKS FAMILIAR.
I DON'T RECOGNIZE IT, SO THEY DON'T MAKE SKATEBOARDS, THAT'S FOR SURE.
KN
WHOEVER IT IS, THEY DON'T WANT OUR PARENTS TO FIND ANY ENDANGERED SPECIES. I WONDER WHY. AND WHAT'S MR. WILEY GOT TO DO WITH IT?
GOT ME. I'M JUST OUT HERE BECAUSE MY DAD WANTED TO SEPARATE ME FROM MY LAPTOP.
LET'S GET BACK BEFORE WILEY BLOWS HIS SPLINT AGAIN.

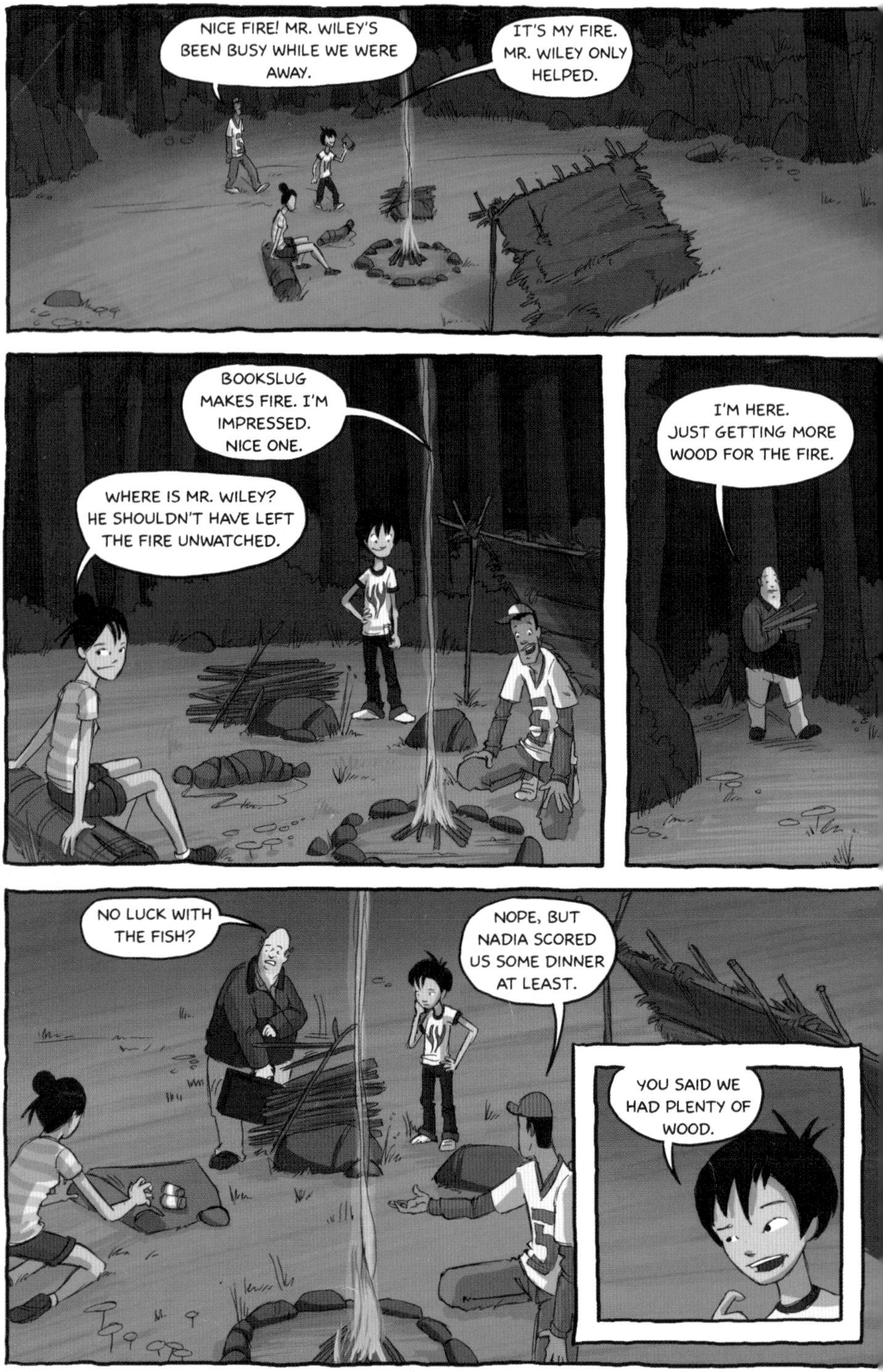

NICE FIRE! MR. WILEY'S BEEN BUSY WHILE WE WERE AWAY.
IT'S MY FIRE. MR. WILEY ONLY HELPED.
BOOKSLUG MAKES FIRE. I'M IMPRESSED. NICE ONE.
WHERE IS MR. WILEY? HE SHOULDN'T HAVE LEFT THE FIRE UNWATCHED.
I'M HERE. JUST GETTING MORE WOOD FOR THE FIRE.
NO LUCK WITH THE FISH?
NOPE, BUT NADIA SCORED US SOME DINNER AT LEAST.
YOU SAID WE HAD PLENTY OF WOOD.

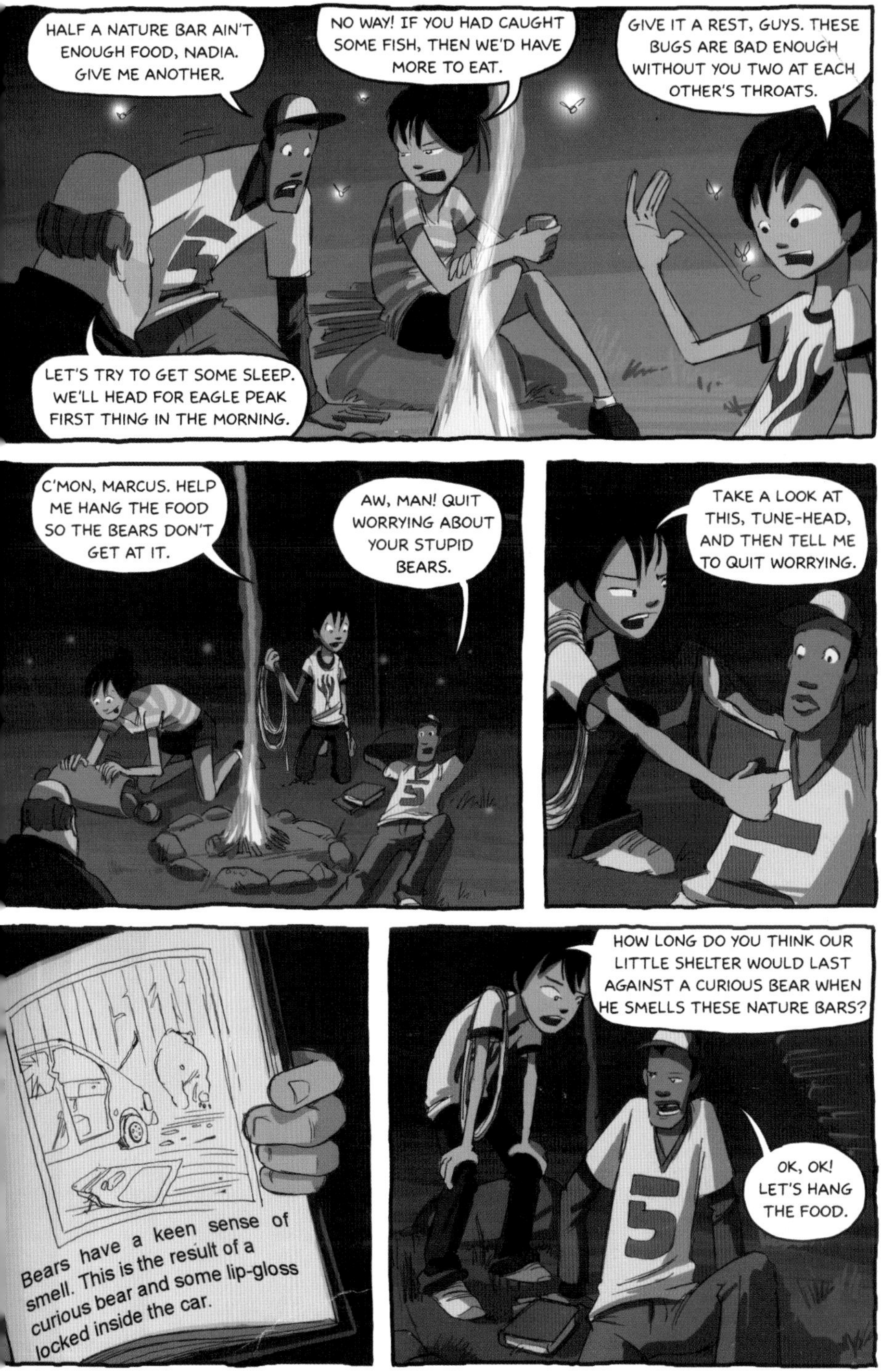
HALF A NATURE BAR AIN'T ENOUGH FOOD, NADIA. GIVE ME ANOTHER.
NO WAY! IF YOU HAD CAUGHT SOME FISH, THEN WE'D HAVE MORE TO EAT.
GIVE IT A REST, GUYS. THESE BUGS ARE BAD ENOUGH WITHOUT YOU TWO AT EACH OTHER'S THROATS.
LET'S TRY TO GET SOME SLEEP. WE'LL HEAD FOR EAGLE PEAK FIRST THING IN THE MORNING.
C'MON, MARCUS. HELP ME HANG THE FOOD SO THE BEARS DON'T GET AT IT.
AW, MAN! QUIT WORRYING ABOUT YOUR STUPID BEARS.
TAKE A LOOK AT THIS, TUNE-HEAD, AND THEN TELL ME TO QUIT WORRYING.
Bears have a keen sense of smell. This is the result of a curious bear and some lip-gloss locked inside the car.
HOW LONG DO YOU THINK OUR LITTLE SHELTER WOULD LAST AGAINST A CURIOUS BEAR WHEN HE SMELLS THESE NATURE BARS?
OK, OK! LET'S HANG THE FOOD.

SORRY ABOUT YELLING AT DEVIN BACK THERE. I SHOULD HAVE THANKED HIM FOR FINDING MY BRIEFCASE.

FORGET IT. HE'S A LITTLE SNOOP. I TOLD HIM TO LEAVE YOUR STUFF ALONE. IT'S PROBABLY VERY IMPORTANT.

JUST BORING GOVERNMENT STUFF. BUT IT'S ALL NEEDED TO MAKE SURE EVERYBODY GETS TO HAVE THEIR SAY ABOUT WHAT TO DO WITH THE BIG HORN VALLEY.

WHO ELSE IS INTERESTED IN THE VALLEY?

LOTS OF PEOPLE. MINING COMPANIES, LOGGING COMPANIES AND CONDO DEVELOPERS ALL WANT A PIECE OF THE VALLEY. AND HABITAT WATCH WANTS EVERYONE TO LEAVE IT ALONE.

AND YOU HELP DECIDE WHO GETS IT ALL. IS THAT WHY SOMEONE IS PUTTING MONEY INTO YOUR BANK ACCOUNT?

SO YOUR TWERP BROTHER TOLD YOU ABOUT THE LETTER? I DESTROYED IT AN HOUR AGO, SO ALL YOU GOT IS THE WORD OF A CONFUSED KID WITH A BAD FEAR OF BEARS.

YOU SURE YOU GOT THE WHOLE LETTER? DEVIN'S FEARS MAY BE BAD, BUT HIS GRIP IS PRETTY GOOD.

YOU'RE UP TO SOMETHING, WILEY. IT'S PROBABLY ILLEGAL, AND IT'LL DEFINITELY RUIN THE VALLEY. WHEN WE GET OUT OF HERE, YOU'LL BE ANSWERING SOME TOUGH QUESTIONS FROM THE POLICE.

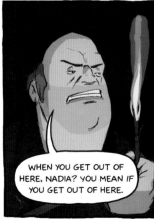

WHEN YOU GET OUT OF HERE, NADIA? YOU MEAN IF YOU GET OUT OF HERE.

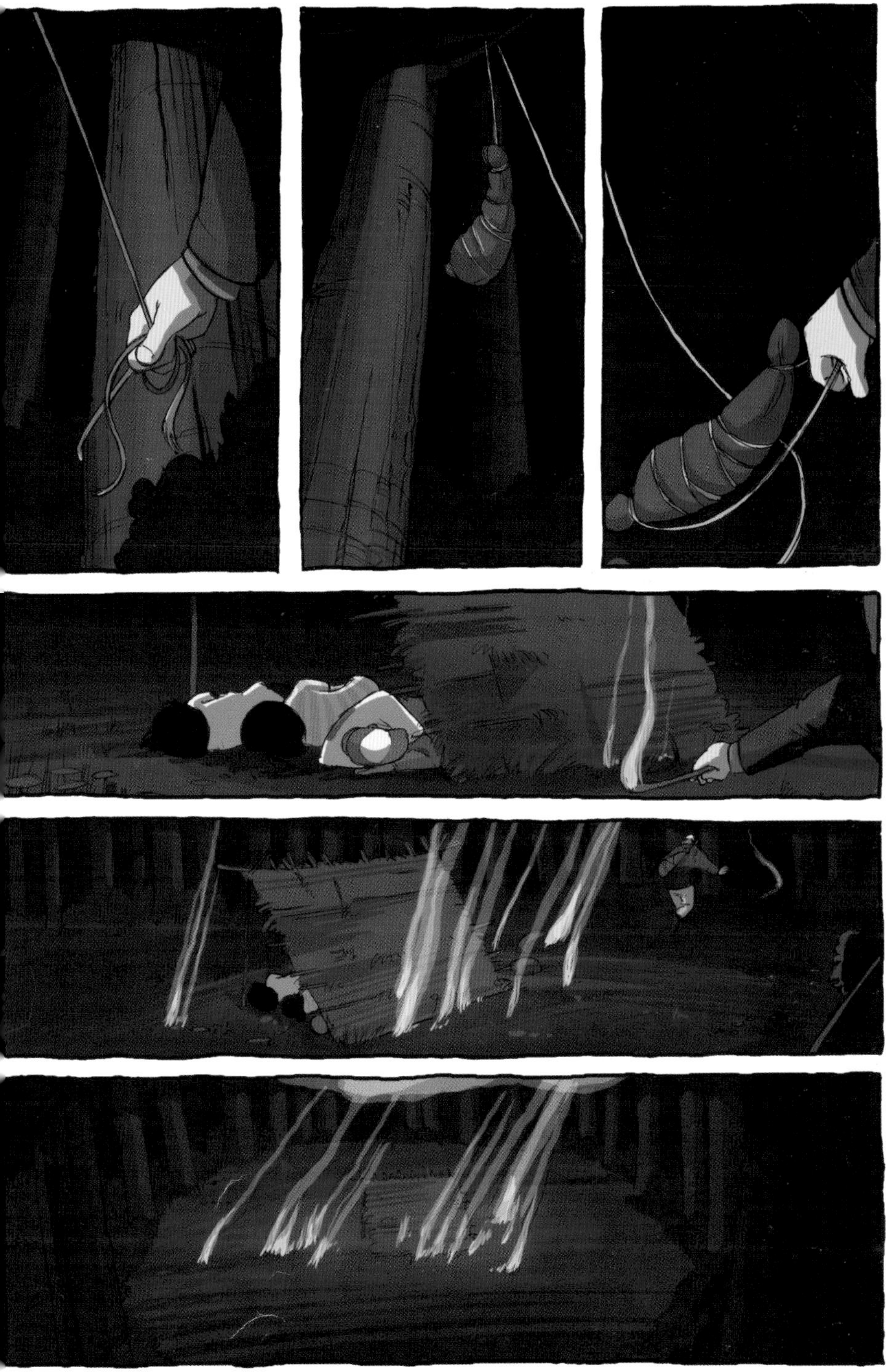

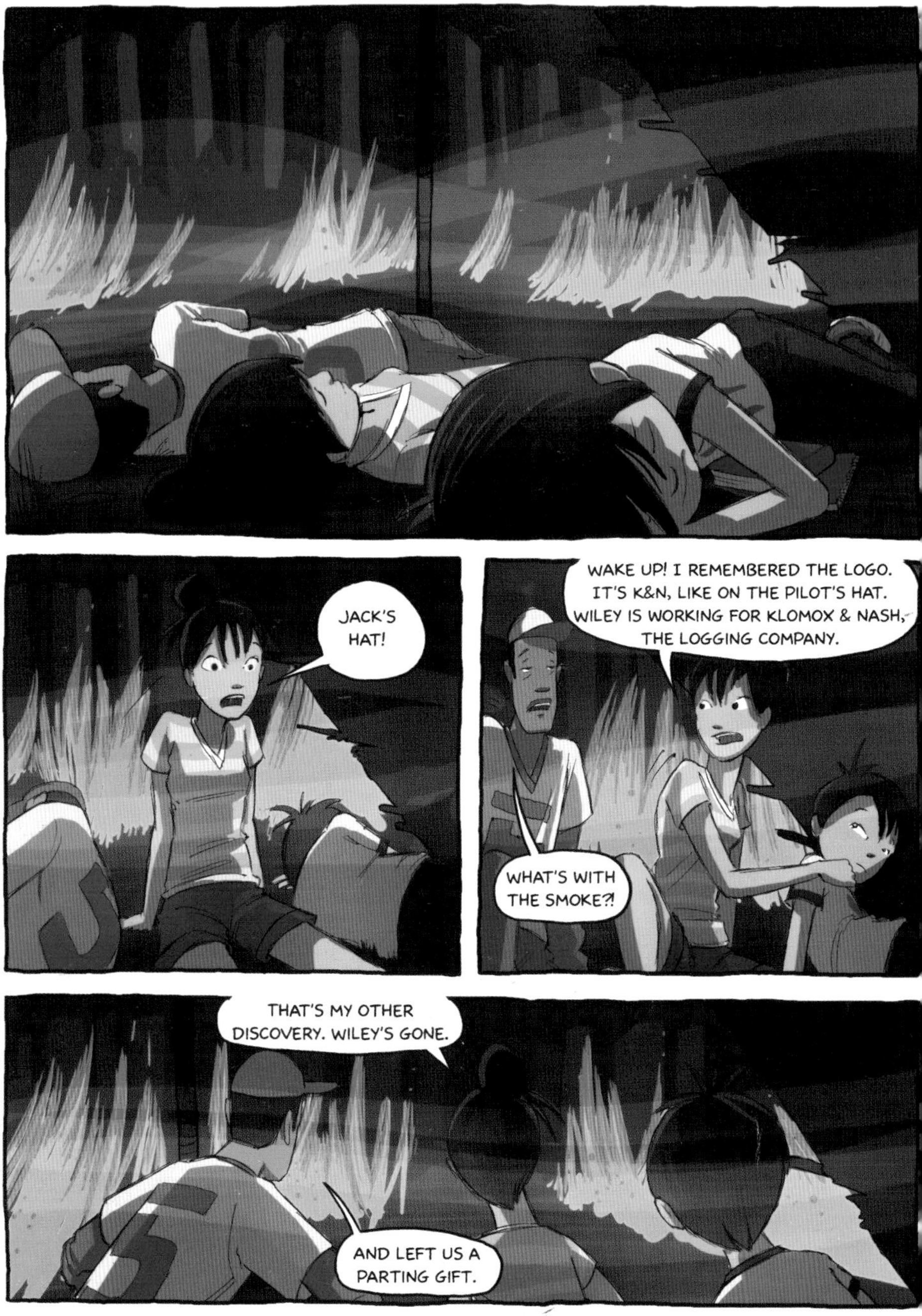
JACK'S HAT!
WAKE UP! I REMEMBERED THE LOGO. IT'S K&N, LIKE ON THE PILOT'S HAT. WILEY IS WORKING FOR KLOMOX & NASH, THE LOGGING COMPANY.
WHAT'S WITH THE SMOKE?!
THAT'S MY OTHER DISCOVERY. WILEY'S GONE.
AND LEFT US A PARTING GIFT.

CHAPTER FOUR

FIERY CROSSING

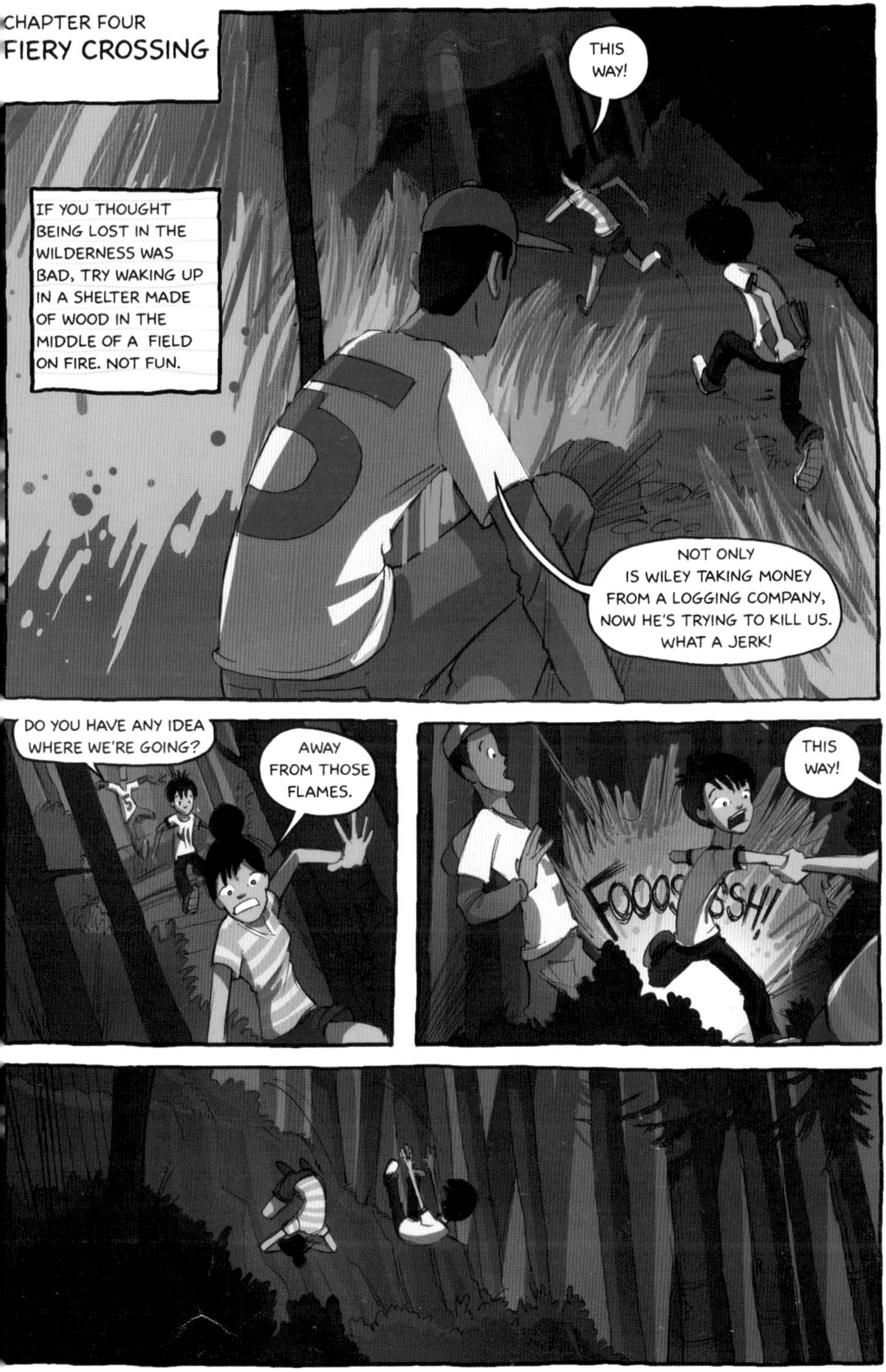

THIS WAY!
IF YOU THOUGHT BEING LOST IN THE WILDERNESS WAS BAD, TRY WAKING UP IN A SHELTER MADE OF WOOD IN THE MIDDLE OF A FIELD ON FIRE. NOT FUN.
NOT ONLY IS WILEY TAKING MONEY FROM A LOGGING COMPANY, NOW HE'S TRYING TO KILL US. WHAT A JERK!
DO YOU HAVE ANY IDEA WHERE WE'RE GOING?
AWAY FROM THOSE FLAMES.
THIS WAY!
FOOOSSSH!

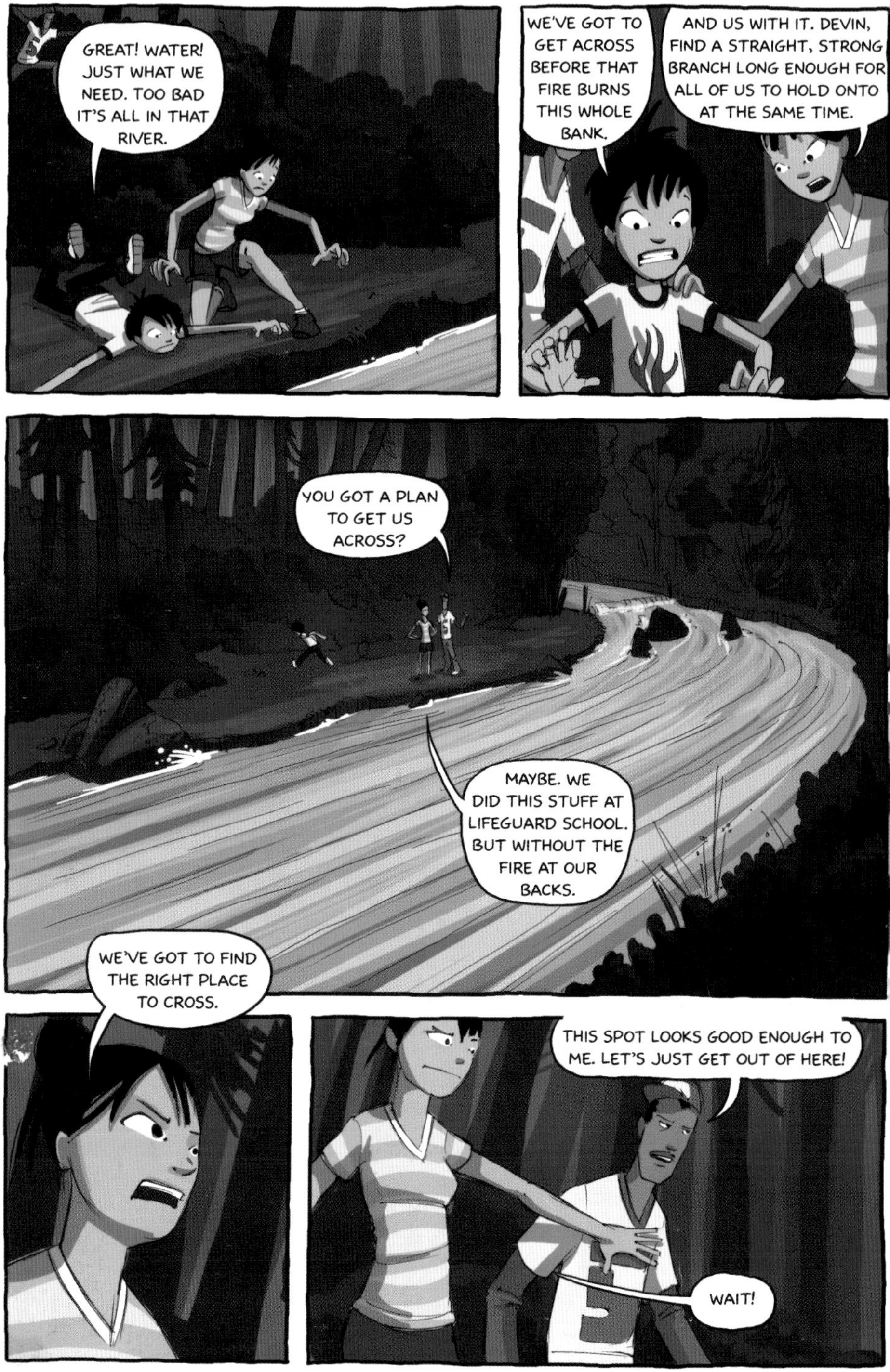
GREAT! WATER! JUST WHAT WE NEED. TOO BAD IT'S ALL IN THAT RIVER.
WE'VE GOT TO GET ACROSS BEFORE THAT FIRE BURNS THIS WHOLE BANK.
AND US WITH IT. DEVIN, FIND A STRAIGHT, STRONG BRANCH LONG ENOUGH FOR ALL OF US TO HOLD ONTO AT THE SAME TIME.
YOU GOT A PLAN TO GET US ACROSS?
MAYBE. WE DID THIS STUFF AT LIFEGUARD SCHOOL. BUT WITHOUT THE FIRE AT OUR BACKS.
WE'VE GOT TO FIND THE RIGHT PLACE TO CROSS.
THIS SPOT LOOKS GOOD ENOUGH TO ME. LET'S JUST GET OUT OF HERE!
WAIT!

RIVERS CAN BE DANGEROUS. ALWAYS STUDY THE SURFACE TO KNOW WHAT'S UNDERNEATH.

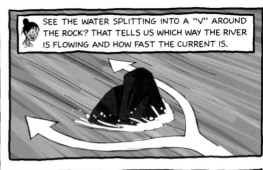

SEE THE WATER SPLITTING INTO A "V" AROUND THE ROCK? THAT TELLS US WHICH WAY THE RIVER IS FLOWING AND HOW FAST THE CURRENT IS.

A WAVE THAT SEEMS TO STAY IN ONE PLACE MEANS THERE'S PROBABLY A BOULDER ON THE RIVER BOTTOM. THE WATER WILL BE SHALLOW THERE, BUT THE CURRENT MIGHT BE TOO STRONG TO CROSS.

IF THE RIVER LOOKS LIKE IT'S FLOWING BACK ON ITSELF - WATCH OUT! THERE'S PROBABLY A STRONG UNDERTOW THAT COULD TRAP YOU AGAINST THE ROCKS.

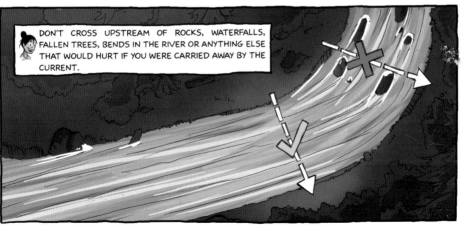

DON'T CROSS UPSTREAM OF ROCKS, WATERFALLS, FALLEN TREES, BENDS IN THE RIVER OR ANYTHING ELSE THAT WOULD HURT IF YOU WERE CARRIED AWAY BY THE CURRENT.

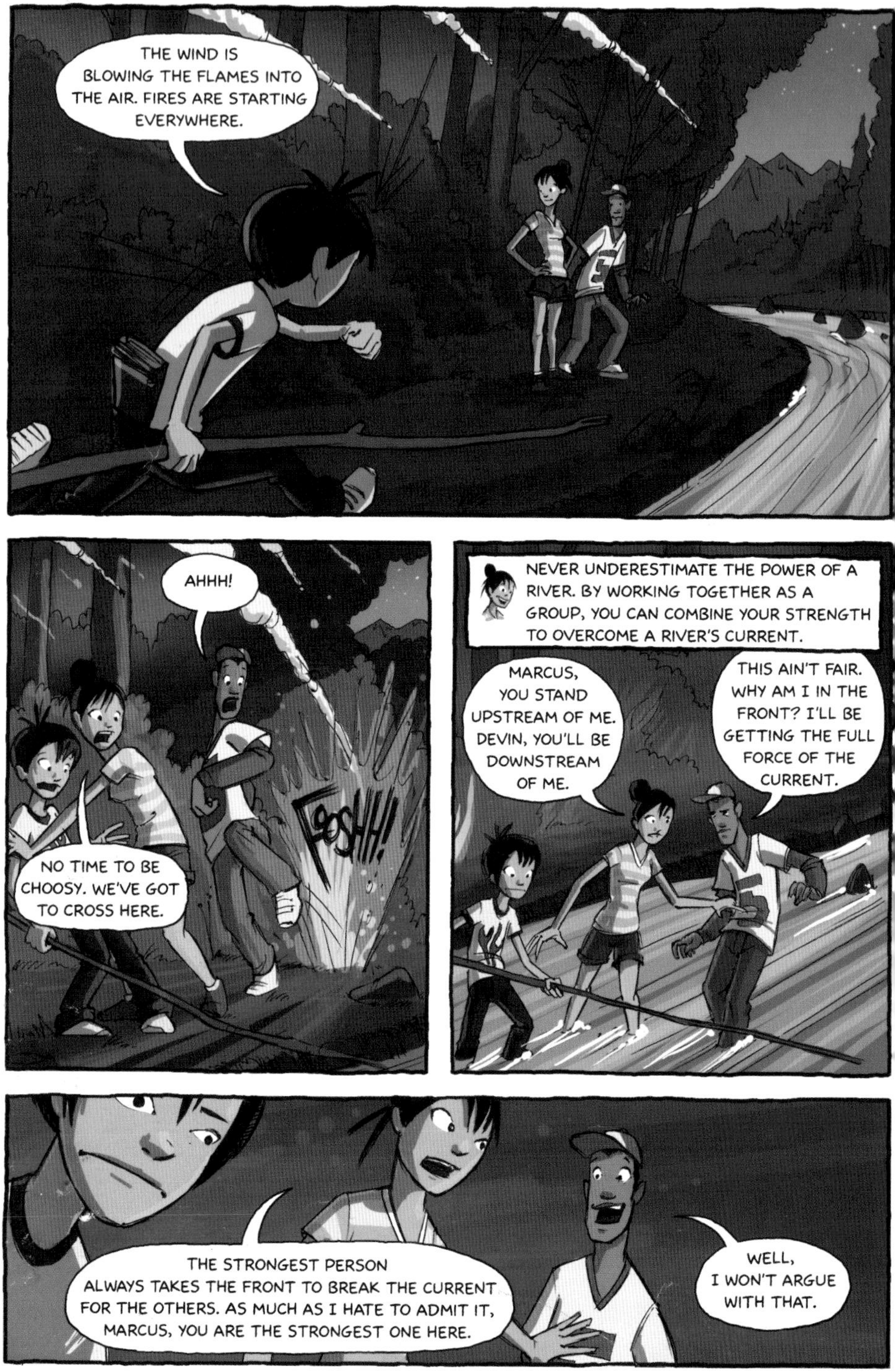
THE WIND IS BLOWING THE FLAMES INTO THE AIR. FIRES ARE STARTING EVERYWHERE.
AHHH!
FOOSHH!
NO TIME TO BE CHOOSY. WE'VE GOT TO CROSS HERE.
NEVER UNDERESTIMATE THE POWER OF A RIVER. BY WORKING TOGETHER AS A GROUP, YOU CAN COMBINE YOUR STRENGTH TO OVERCOME A RIVER'S CURRENT.
MARCUS, YOU STAND UPSTREAM OF ME. DEVIN, YOU'LL BE DOWNSTREAM OF ME.
THIS AIN'T FAIR. WHY AM I IN THE FRONT? I'LL BE GETTING THE FULL FORCE OF THE CURRENT.
THE STRONGEST PERSON ALWAYS TAKES THE FRONT TO BREAK THE CURRENT FOR THE OTHERS. AS MUCH AS I HATE TO ADMIT IT, MARCUS, YOU ARE THE STRONGEST ONE HERE.
WELL, I WON'T ARGUE WITH THAT.

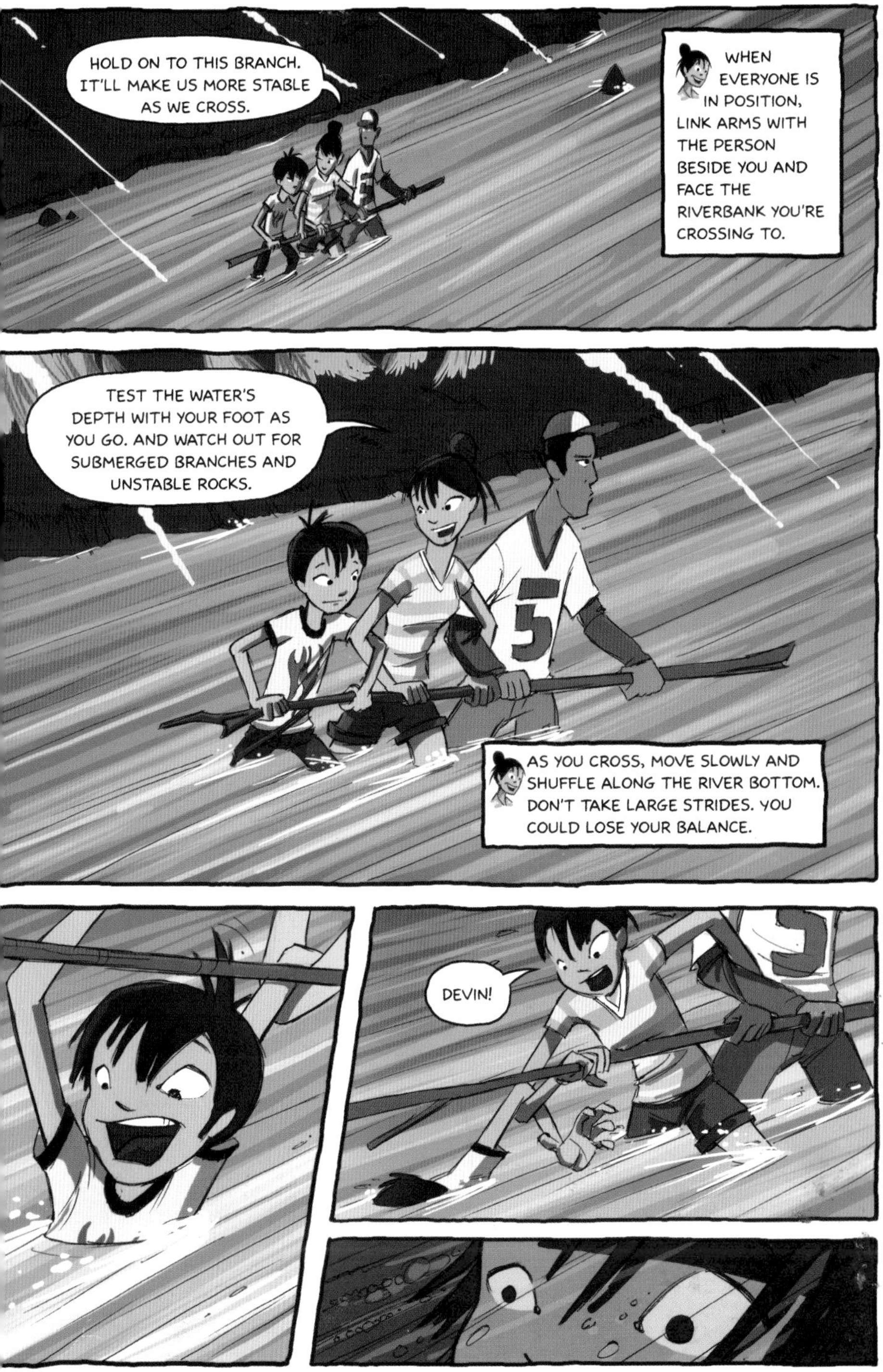
HOLD ON TO THIS BRANCH. IT'LL MAKE US MORE STABLE AS WE CROSS.
WHEN EVERYONE IS IN POSITION, LINK ARMS WITH THE PERSON BESIDE YOU AND FACE THE RIVERBANK YOU'RE CROSSING TO.
TEST THE WATER'S DEPTH WITH YOUR FOOT AS YOU GO. AND WATCH OUT FOR SUBMERGED BRANCHES AND UNSTABLE ROCKS.
AS YOU CROSS, MOVE SLOWLY AND SHUFFLE ALONG THE RIVER BOTTOM. DON'T TAKE LARGE STRIDES. YOU COULD LOSE YOUR BALANCE.
DEVIN!

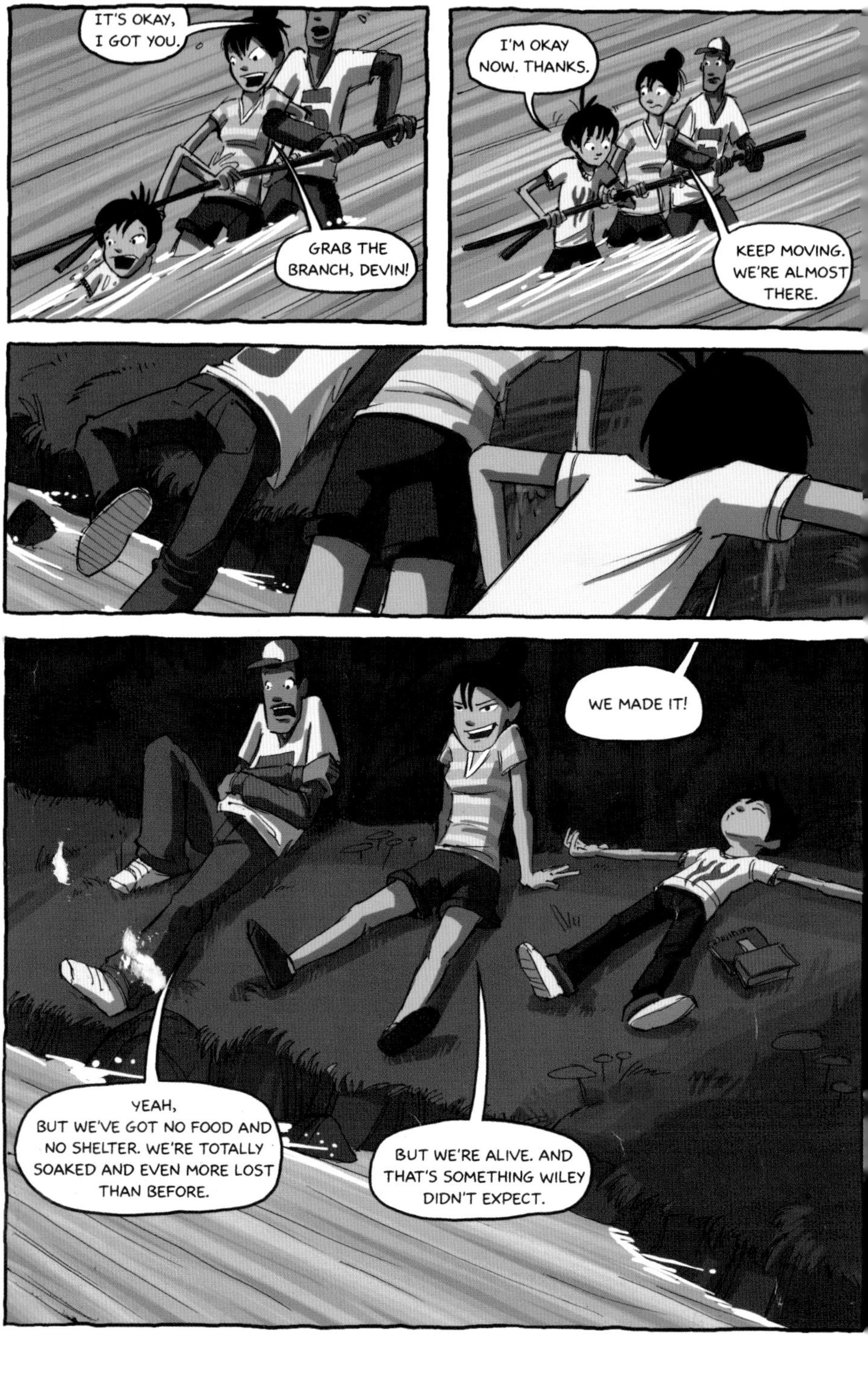
IT'S OKAY, I GOT YOU.
GRAB THE BRANCH, DEVIN!
I'M OKAY NOW. THANKS.
KEEP MOVING. WE'RE ALMOST THERE.
WE MADE IT!
YEAH, BUT WE'VE GOT NO FOOD AND NO SHELTER. WE'RE TOTALLY SOAKED AND EVEN MORE LOST THAN BEFORE.
BUT WE'RE ALIVE. AND THAT'S SOMETHING WILEY DIDN'T EXPECT.

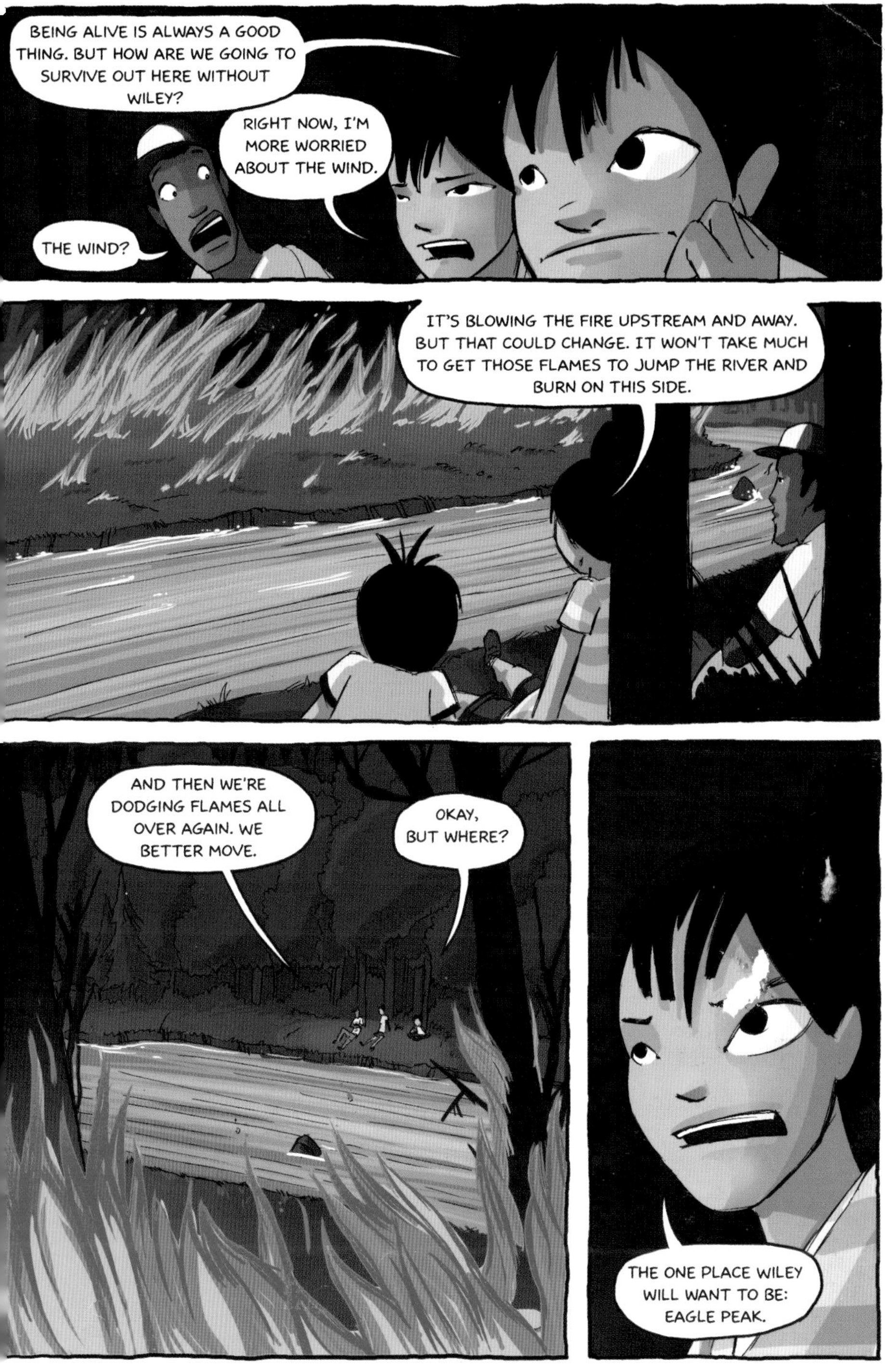
BEING ALIVE IS ALWAYS A GOOD THING. BUT HOW ARE WE GOING TO SURVIVE OUT HERE WITHOUT WILEY?
RIGHT NOW, I'M MORE WORRIED ABOUT THE WIND.
THE WIND?
IT'S BLOWING THE FIRE UPSTREAM AND AWAY. BUT THAT COULD CHANGE. IT WON'T TAKE MUCH TO GET THOSE FLAMES TO JUMP THE RIVER AND BURN ON THIS SIDE.
AND THEN WE'RE DODGING FLAMES ALL OVER AGAIN. WE BETTER MOVE.
OKAY, BUT WHERE?
THE ONE PLACE WILEY WILL WANT TO BE: EAGLE PEAK.

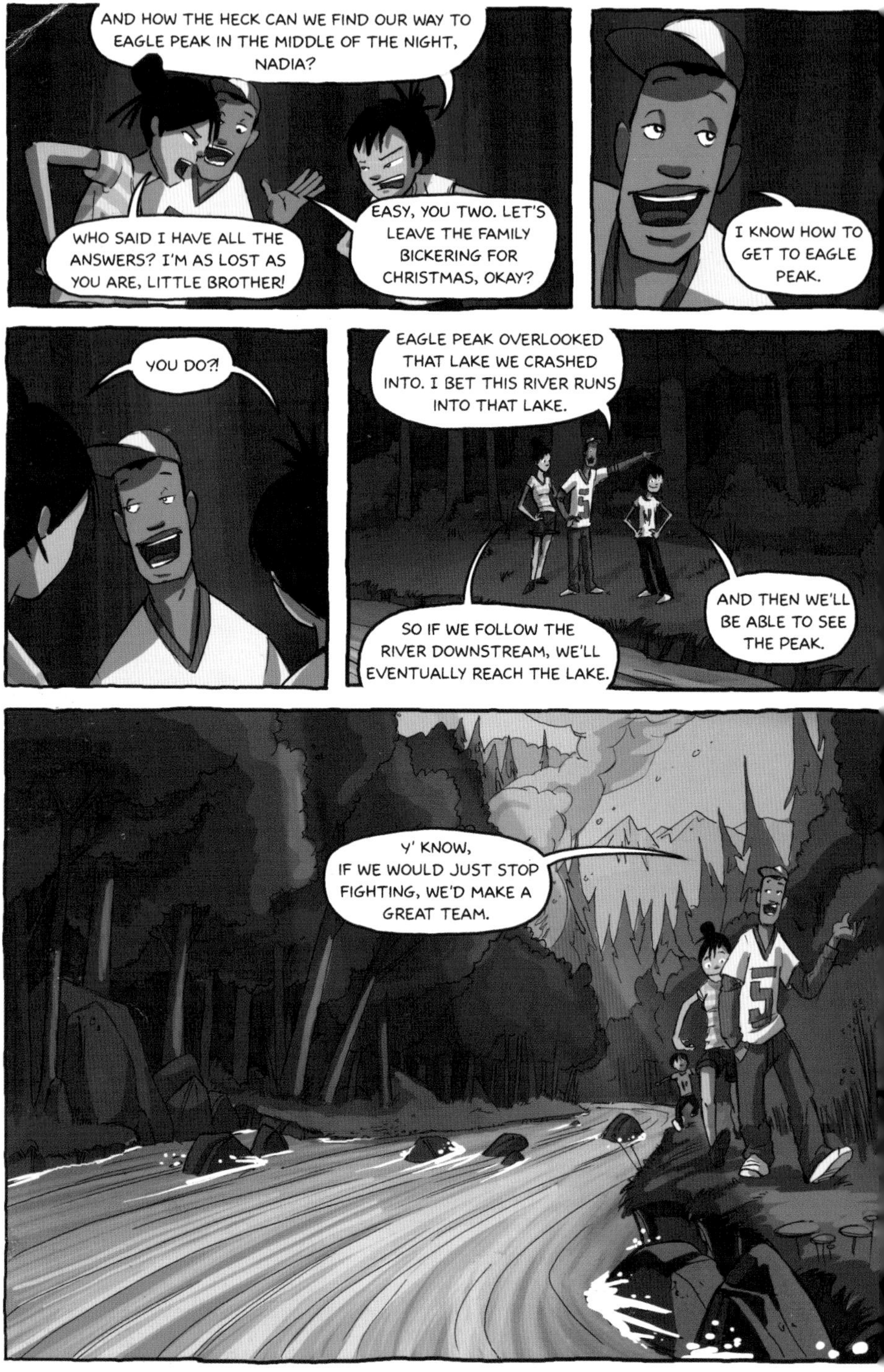
AND HOW THE HECK CAN WE FIND OUR WAY TO EAGLE PEAK IN THE MIDDLE OF THE NIGHT, NADIA?
WHO SAID I HAVE ALL THE ANSWERS? I'M AS LOST AS YOU ARE, LITTLE BROTHER!
EASY, YOU TWO. LET'S LEAVE THE FAMILY BICKERING FOR CHRISTMAS, OKAY?
I KNOW HOW TO GET TO EAGLE PEAK.
YOU DO?!
EAGLE PEAK OVERLOOKED THAT LAKE WE CRASHED INTO. I BET THIS RIVER RUNS INTO THAT LAKE.
SO IF WE FOLLOW THE RIVER DOWNSTREAM, WE'LL EVENTUALLY REACH THE LAKE.
AND THEN WE'LL BE ABLE TO SEE THE PEAK.
Y' KNOW, IF WE WOULD JUST STOP FIGHTING, WE'D MAKE A GREAT TEAM.

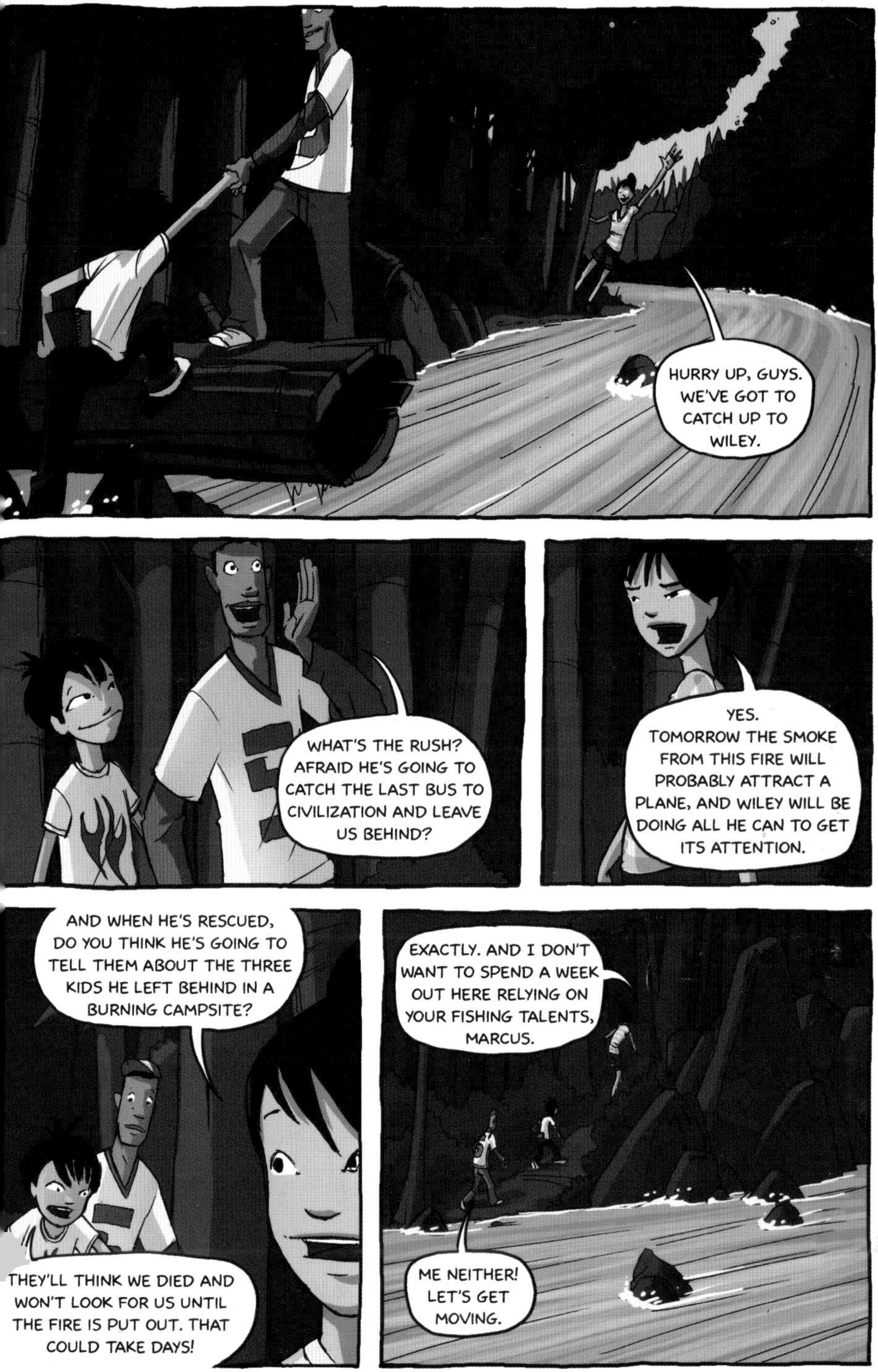
HURRY UP, GUYS. WE'VE GOT TO CATCH UP TO WILEY.
WHAT'S THE RUSH? AFRAID HE'S GOING TO CATCH THE LAST BUS TO CIVILIZATION AND LEAVE US BEHIND?
YES. TOMORROW THE SMOKE FROM THIS FIRE WILL PROBABLY ATTRACT A PLANE, AND WILEY WILL BE DOING ALL HE CAN TO GET ITS ATTENTION.
AND WHEN HE'S RESCUED, DO YOU THINK HE'S GOING TO TELL THEM ABOUT THE THREE KIDS HE LEFT BEHIND IN A BURNING CAMPSITE?
THEY'LL THINK WE DIED AND WON'T LOOK FOR US UNTIL THE FIRE IS PUT OUT. THAT COULD TAKE DAYS!
EXACTLY. AND I DON'T WANT TO SPEND A WEEK OUT HERE RELYING ON YOUR FISHING TALENTS, MARCUS.
ME NEITHER! LET'S GET MOVING.

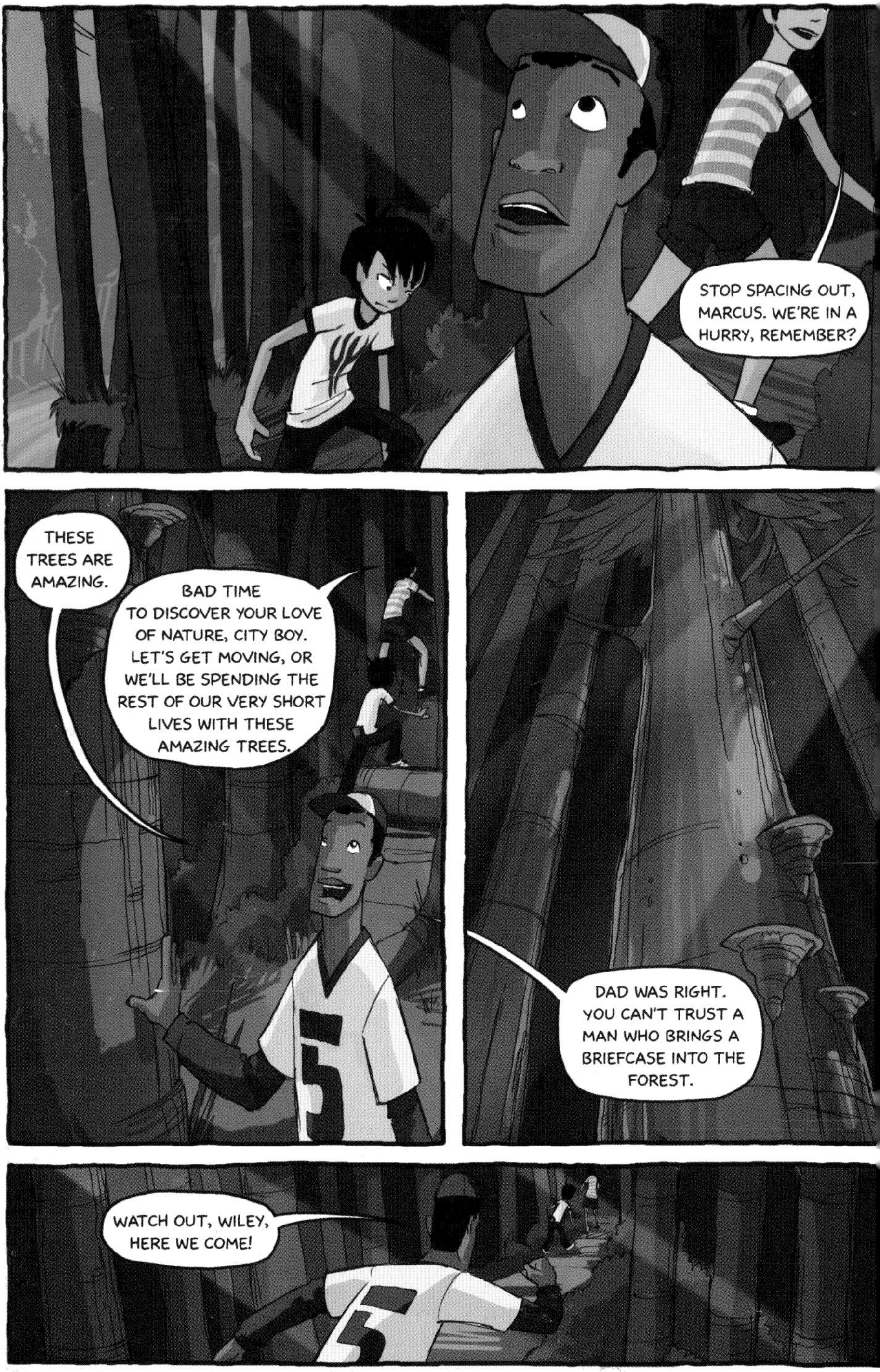
STOP SPACING OUT, MARCUS. WE'RE IN A HURRY, REMEMBER?
THESE TREES ARE AMAZING.
BAD TIME TO DISCOVER YOUR LOVE OF NATURE, CITY BOY. LET'S GET MOVING, OR WE'LL BE SPENDING THE REST OF OUR VERY SHORT LIVES WITH THESE AMAZING TREES.
DAD WAS RIGHT. YOU CAN'T TRUST A MAN WHO BRINGS A BRIEFCASE INTO THE FOREST.
WATCH OUT, WILEY, HERE WE COME!

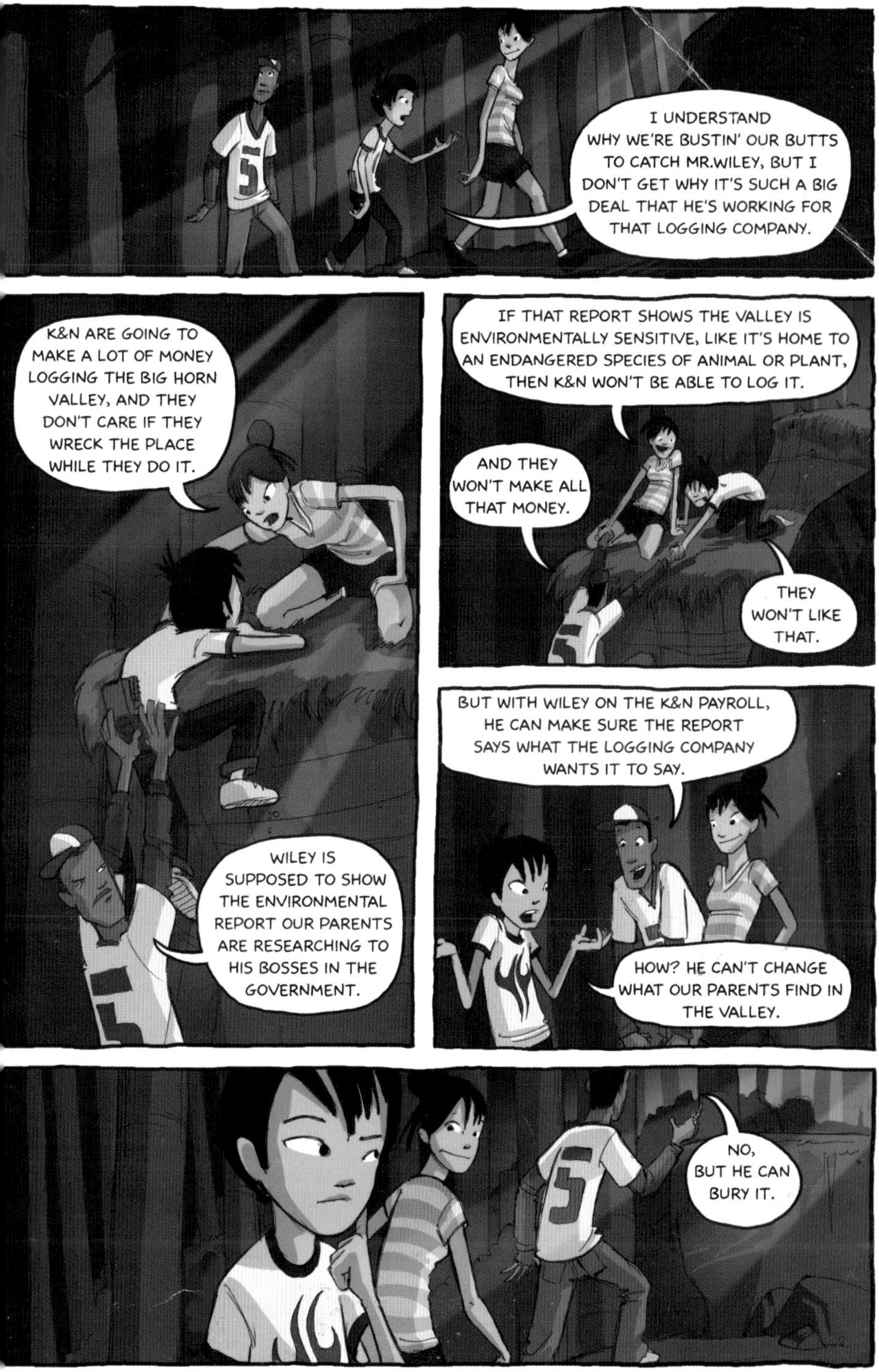
I UNDERSTAND WHY WE'RE BUSTIN' OUR BUTTS TO CATCH MR.WILEY, BUT I DON'T GET WHY IT'S SUCH A BIG DEAL THAT HE'S WORKING FOR THAT LOGGING COMPANY.
K&N ARE GOING TO MAKE A LOT OF MONEY LOGGING THE BIG HORN VALLEY, AND THEY DON'T CARE IF THEY WRECK THE PLACE WHILE THEY DO IT.
WILEY IS SUPPOSED TO SHOW THE ENVIRONMENTAL REPORT OUR PARENTS ARE RESEARCHING TO HIS BOSSES IN THE GOVERNMENT.
IF THAT REPORT SHOWS THE VALLEY IS ENVIRONMENTALLY SENSITIVE, LIKE IT'S HOME TO AN ENDANGERED SPECIES OF ANIMAL OR PLANT, THEN K&N WON'T BE ABLE TO LOG IT.
AND THEY WON'T MAKE ALL THAT MONEY.
THEY WON'T LIKE THAT.
BUT WITH WILEY ON THE K&N PAYROLL, HE CAN MAKE SURE THE REPORT SAYS WHAT THE LOGGING COMPANY WANTS IT TO SAY.
HOW? HE CAN'T CHANGE WHAT OUR PARENTS FIND IN THE VALLEY.
NO, BUT HE CAN BURY IT.

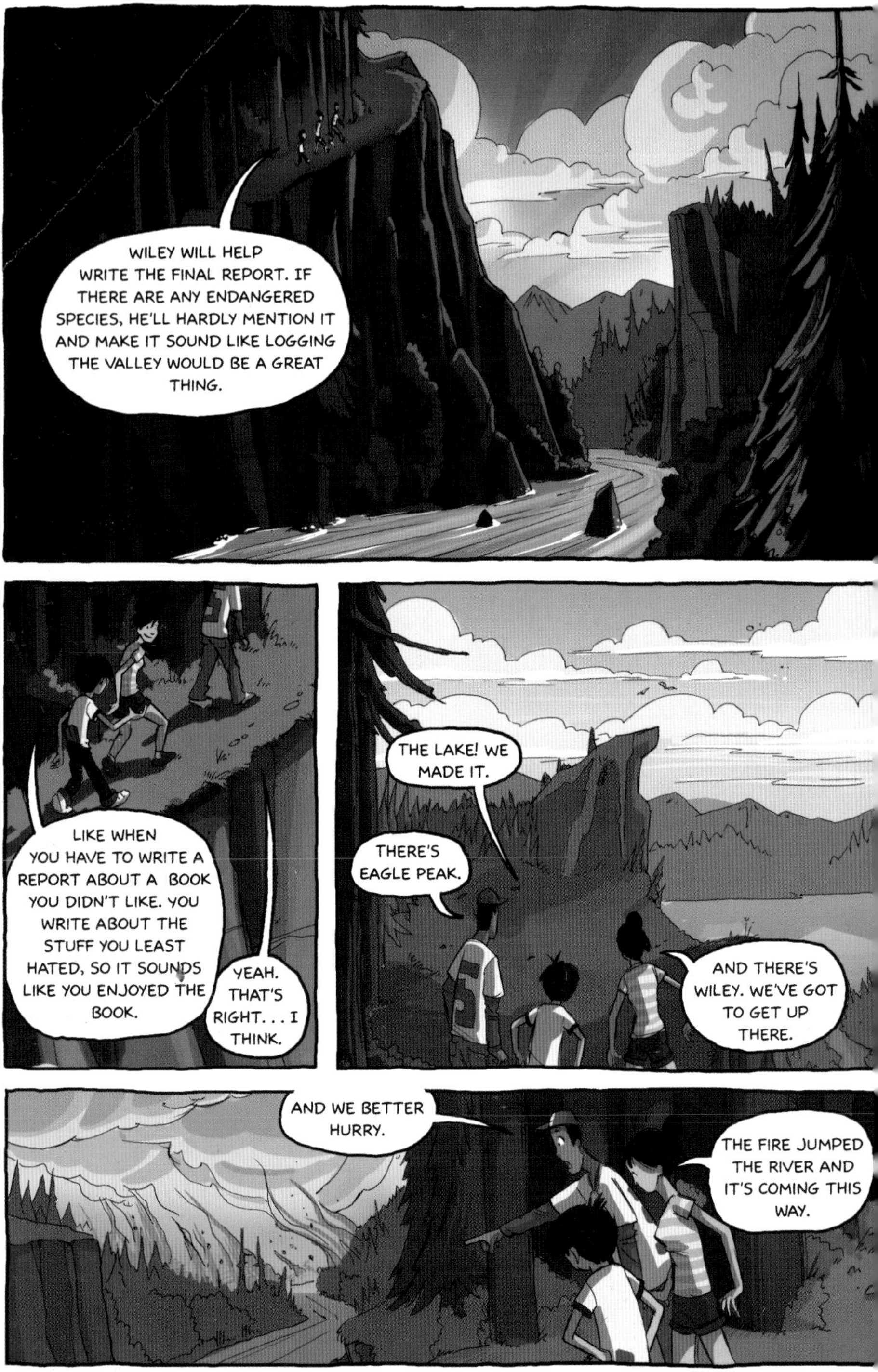
WILEY WILL HELP WRITE THE FINAL REPORT. IF THERE ARE ANY ENDANGERED SPECIES, HE'LL HARDLY MENTION IT AND MAKE IT SOUND LIKE LOGGING THE VALLEY WOULD BE A GREAT THING.
LIKE WHEN YOU HAVE TO WRITE A REPORT ABOUT A BOOK YOU DIDN'T LIKE. YOU WRITE ABOUT THE STUFF YOU LEAST HATED, SO IT SOUNDS LIKE YOU ENJOYED THE BOOK.
YEAH. THAT'S RIGHT. . . I THINK.
THE LAKE! WE MADE IT.
THERE'S EAGLE PEAK.
AND THERE'S WILEY. WE'VE GOT TO GET UP THERE.
AND WE BETTER HURRY.
THE FIRE JUMPED THE RIVER AND IT'S COMING THIS WAY.

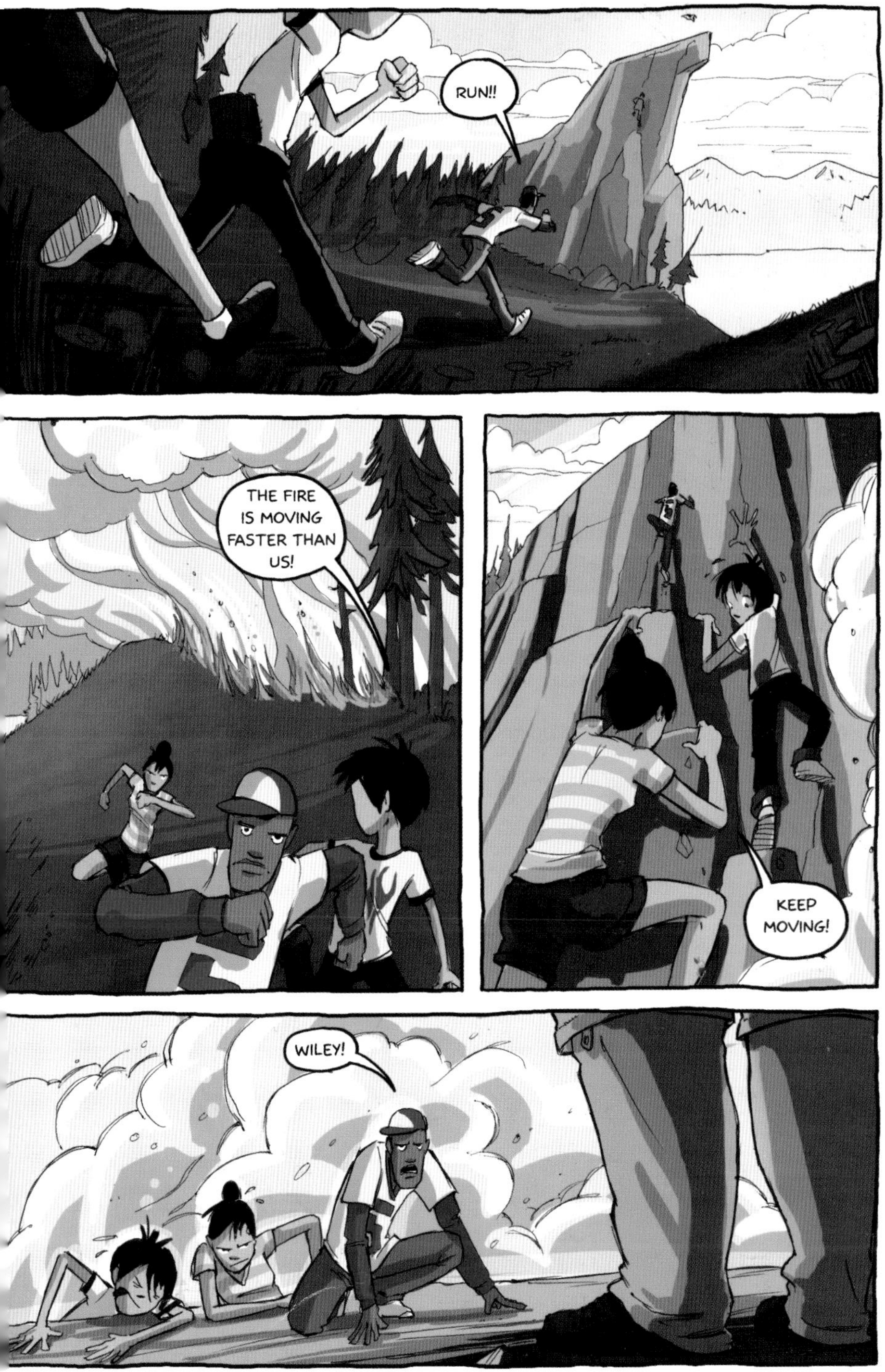
RUN!!
THE FIRE IS MOVING FASTER THAN US!
KEEP MOVING!
WILEY!

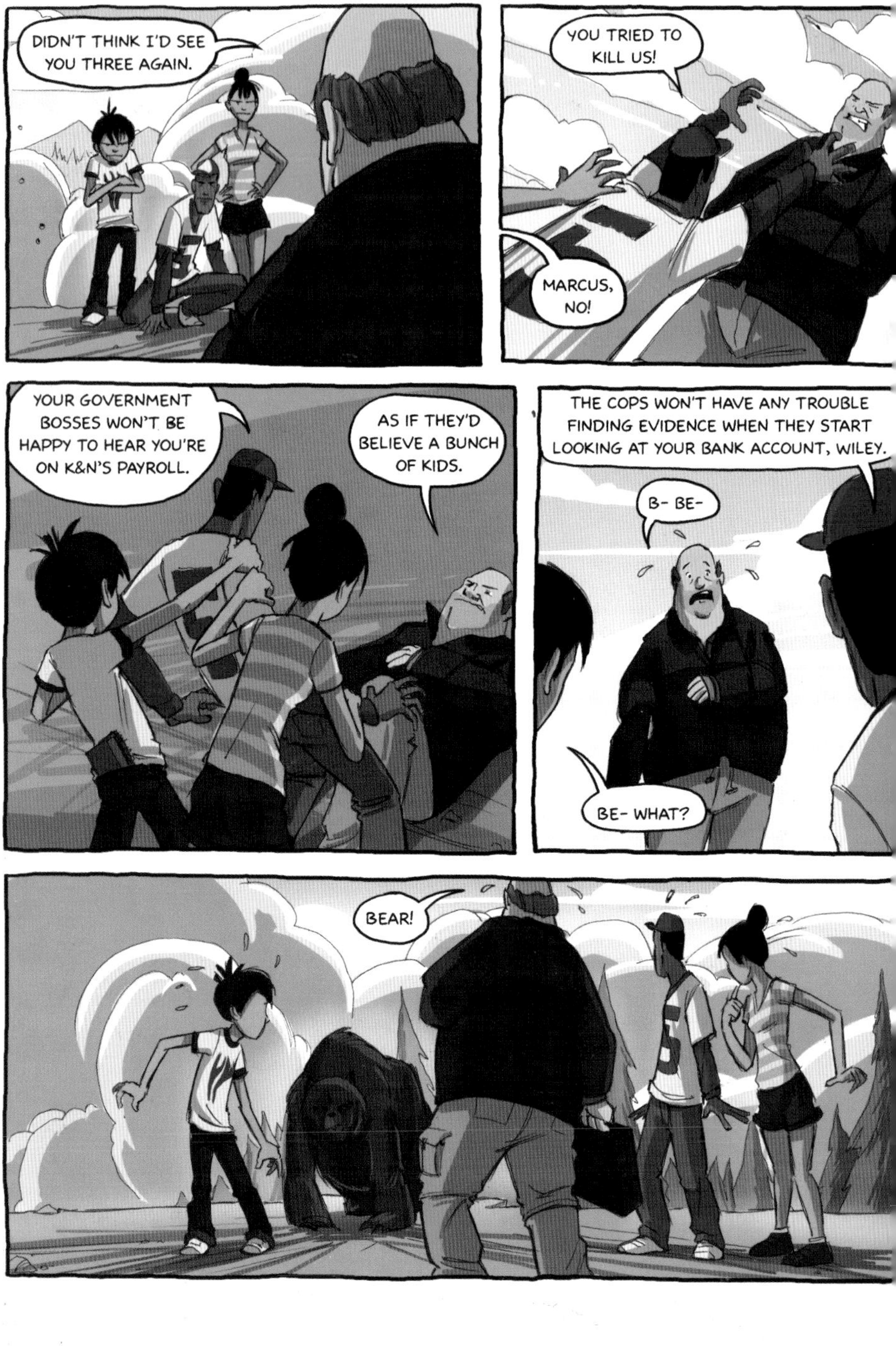
DIDN'T THINK I'D SEE YOU THREE AGAIN.
YOU TRIED TO KILL US!
MARCUS, NO!
YOUR GOVERNMENT BOSSES WON'T BE HAPPY TO HEAR YOU'RE ON K&N'S PAYROLL.
AS IF THEY'D BELIEVE A BUNCH OF KIDS.
THE COPS WON'T HAVE ANY TROUBLE FINDING EVIDENCE WHEN THEY START LOOKING AT YOUR BANK ACCOUNT, WILEY.
B- BE-
BE- WHAT?
BEAR!

CHAPTER FIVE
BEAR DANCING ON EAGLE PEAK

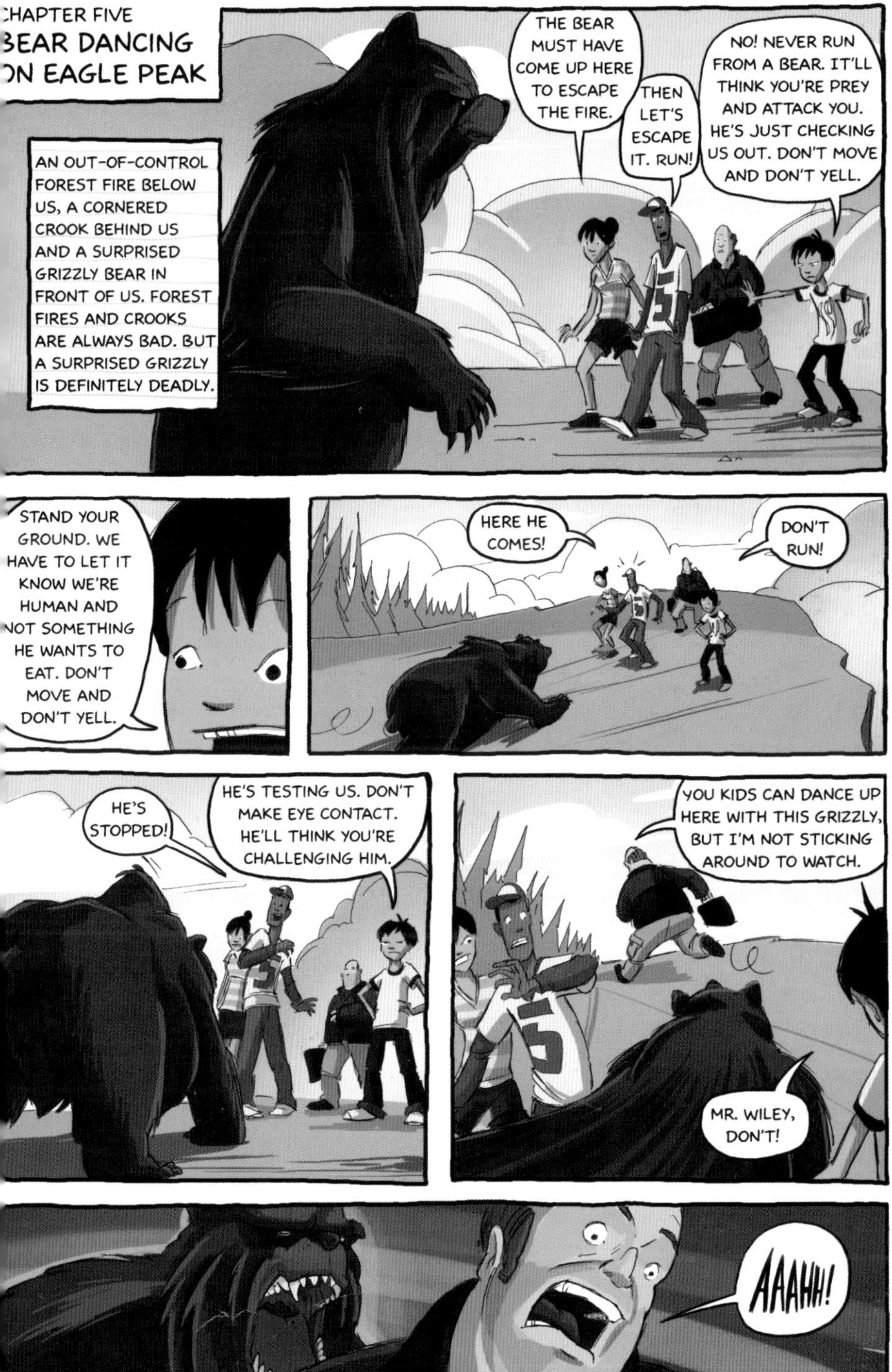
AN OUT-OF-CONTROL FOREST FIRE BELOW US, A CORNERED CROOK BEHIND US AND A SURPRISED GRIZZLY BEAR IN FRONT OF US. FOREST FIRES AND CROOKS ARE ALWAYS BAD. BUT A SURPRISED GRIZZLY IS DEFINITELY DEADLY.
THE BEAR MUST HAVE COME UP HERE TO ESCAPE THE FIRE.
THEN LET'S ESCAPE IT. RUN!
NO! NEVER RUN FROM A BEAR. IT'LL THINK YOU'RE PREY AND ATTACK YOU. HE'S JUST CHECKING US OUT. DON'T MOVE AND DON'T YELL.
STAND YOUR GROUND. WE HAVE TO LET IT KNOW WE'RE HUMAN AND NOT SOMETHING HE WANTS TO EAT. DON'T MOVE AND DON'T YELL.
HERE HE COMES!
DON'T RUN!
HE'S STOPPED!
HE'S TESTING US. DON'T MAKE EYE CONTACT. HE'LL THINK YOU'RE CHALLENGING HIM.
YOU KIDS CAN DANCE UP HERE WITH THIS GRIZZLY, BUT I'M NOT STICKING AROUND TO WATCH.
MR. WILEY, DON'T!
AAAHH!

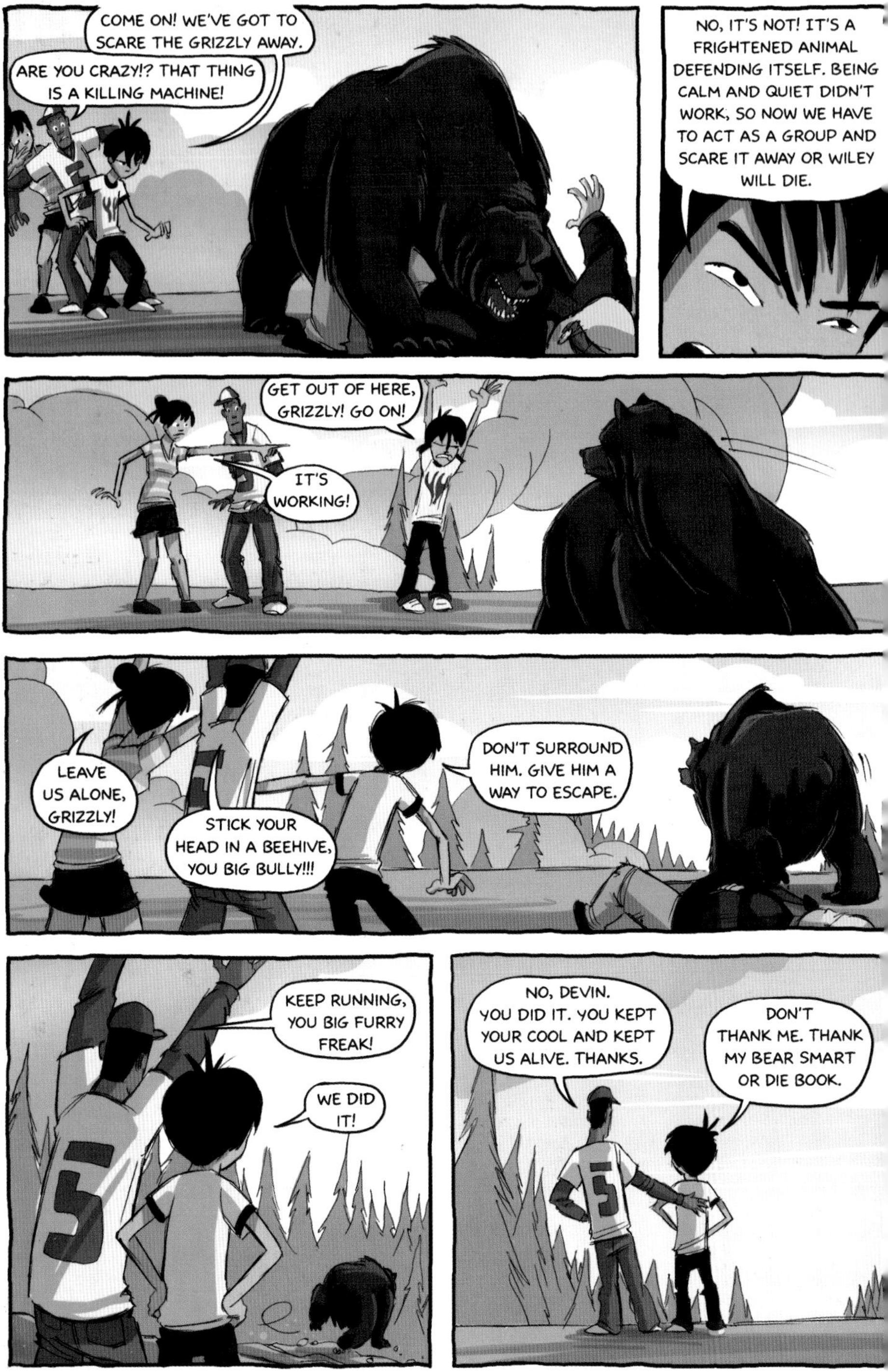
COME ON! WE'VE GOT TO SCARE THE GRIZZLY AWAY.
ARE YOU CRAZY!? THAT THING IS A KILLING MACHINE!
NO, IT'S NOT! IT'S A FRIGHTENED ANIMAL DEFENDING ITSELF. BEING CALM AND QUIET DIDN'T WORK, SO NOW WE HAVE TO ACT AS A GROUP AND SCARE IT AWAY OR WILEY WILL DIE.
GET OUT OF HERE, GRIZZLY! GO ON!
IT'S WORKING!
LEAVE US ALONE, GRIZZLY!
STICK YOUR HEAD IN A BEEHIVE, YOU BIG BULLY!!!
DON'T SURROUND HIM. GIVE HIM A WAY TO ESCAPE.
KEEP RUNNING, YOU BIG FURRY FREAK!
WE DID IT!
NO, DEVIN. YOU DID IT. YOU KEPT YOUR COOL AND KEPT US ALIVE. THANKS.
DON'T THANK ME. THANK MY BEAR SMART OR DIE BOOK.

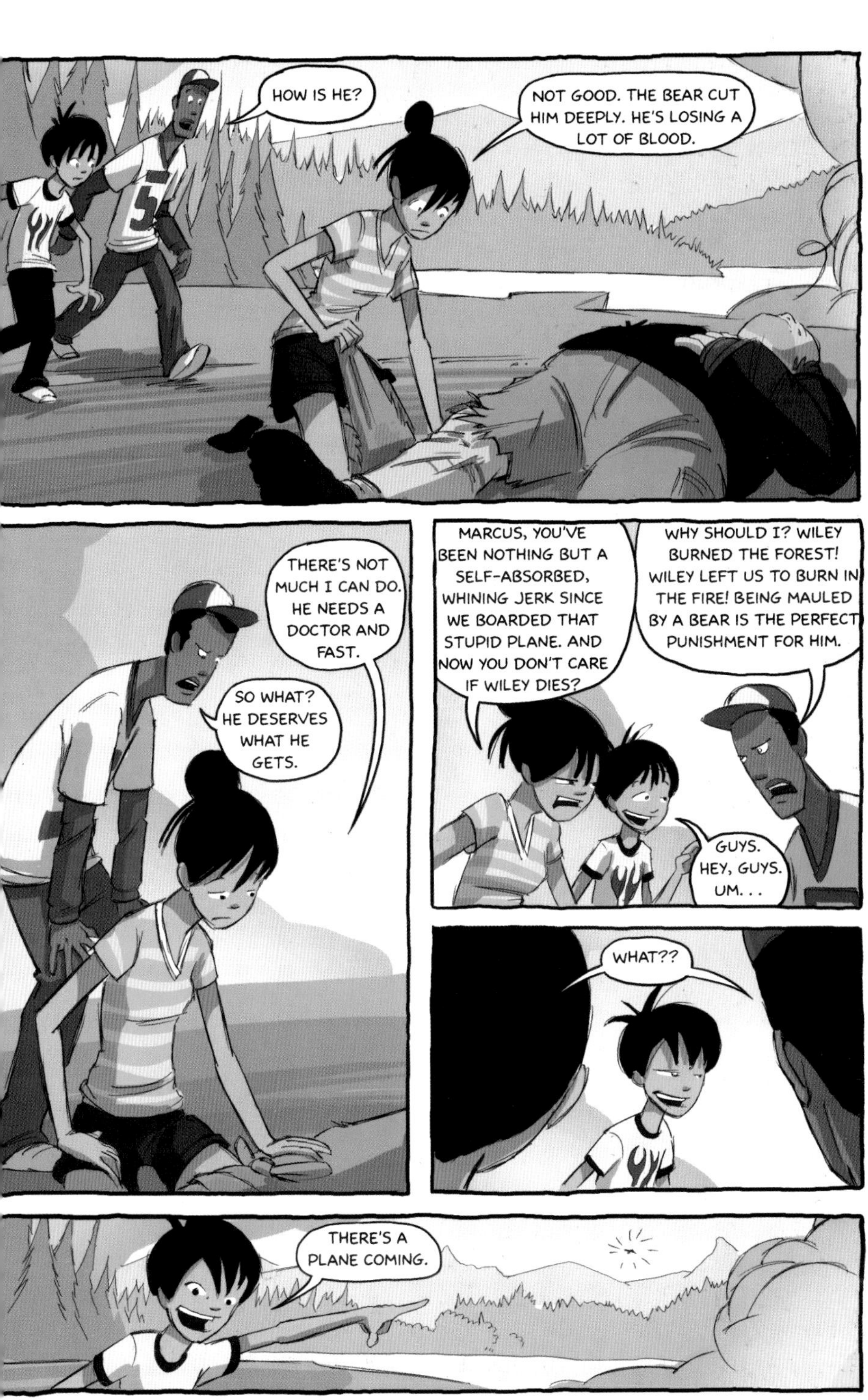
HOW IS HE?
NOT GOOD. THE BEAR CUT HIM DEEPLY. HE'S LOSING A LOT OF BLOOD.
THERE'S NOT MUCH I CAN DO. HE NEEDS A DOCTOR AND FAST.
SO WHAT? HE DESERVES WHAT HE GETS.
MARCUS, YOU'VE BEEN NOTHING BUT A SELF-ABSORBED, WHINING JERK SINCE WE BOARDED THAT STUPID PLANE. AND NOW YOU DON'T CARE IF WILEY DIES?
WHY SHOULD I? WILEY BURNED THE FOREST! WILEY LEFT US TO BURN IN THE FIRE! BEING MAULED BY A BEAR IS THE PERFECT PUNISHMENT FOR HIM.
GUYS. HEY, GUYS. UM. . .
WHAT??
THERE'S A PLANE COMING.

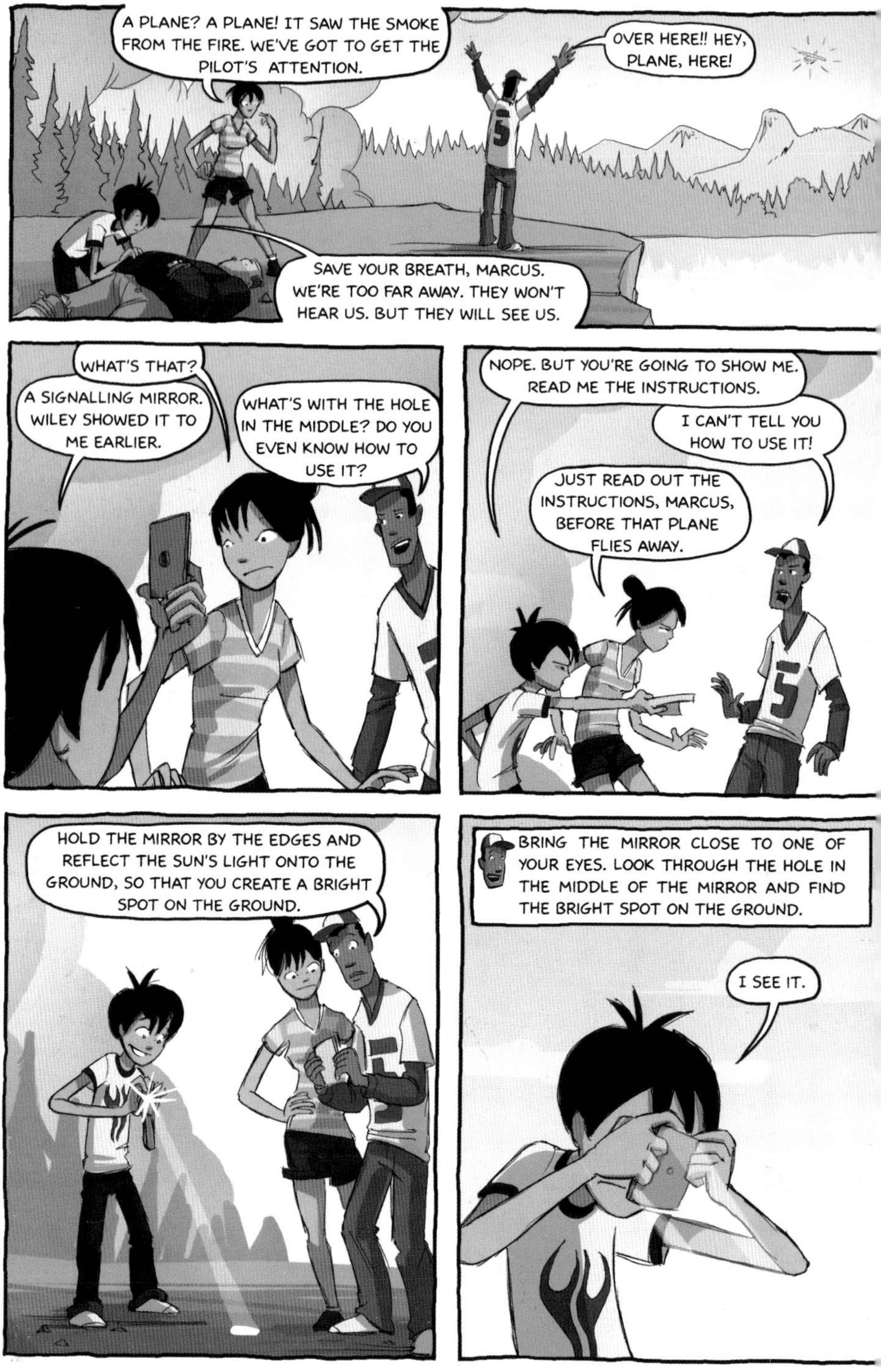
A PLANE? A PLANE! IT SAW THE SMOKE FROM THE FIRE. WE'VE GOT TO GET THE PILOT'S ATTENTION.
OVER HERE!! HEY, PLANE, HERE!
SAVE YOUR BREATH, MARCUS. WE'RE TOO FAR AWAY. THEY WON'T HEAR US. BUT THEY WILL SEE US.
WHAT'S THAT?
A SIGNALLING MIRROR. WILEY SHOWED IT TO ME EARLIER.
WHAT'S WITH THE HOLE IN THE MIDDLE? DO YOU EVEN KNOW HOW TO USE IT?
NOPE. BUT YOU'RE GOING TO SHOW ME. READ ME THE INSTRUCTIONS.
I CAN'T TELL YOU HOW TO USE IT!
JUST READ OUT THE INSTRUCTIONS, MARCUS, BEFORE THAT PLANE FLIES AWAY.
HOLD THE MIRROR BY THE EDGES AND REFLECT THE SUN'S LIGHT ONTO THE GROUND, SO THAT YOU CREATE A BRIGHT SPOT ON THE GROUND.
BRING THE MIRROR CLOSE TO ONE OF YOUR EYES. LOOK THROUGH THE HOLE IN THE MIDDLE OF THE MIRROR AND FIND THE BRIGHT SPOT ON THE GROUND.
I SEE IT.

CONTINUE LOOKING THROUGH THE HOLE IN THE MIRROR AND CAREFULLY BRING THE MIRROR UP TO THE SKY, KEEPING THE BRIGHT SPOT ON THE MESH OF THE HOLE.

TILT AND TURN THE MIRROR UNTIL YOU CAN SEE THE AIRCRAFT IN THE CLEAR PART OF THE HOLE.

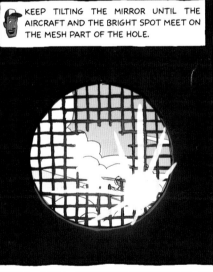

KEEP TILTING THE MIRROR UNTIL THE AIRCRAFT AND THE BRIGHT SPOT MEET ON THE MESH PART OF THE HOLE.

GOT IT!

WIGGLE THE MIRROR SO THAT THE BRIGHT SPOT MOVES ALONG THE AIRCRAFT. THIS WILL CREATE A FLASHING EFFECT, WHICH WILL ATTRACT THE PILOT'S ATTENTION.

KEEP WIGGLING, DEVIN. THAT PILOT HAS TO SEE US.

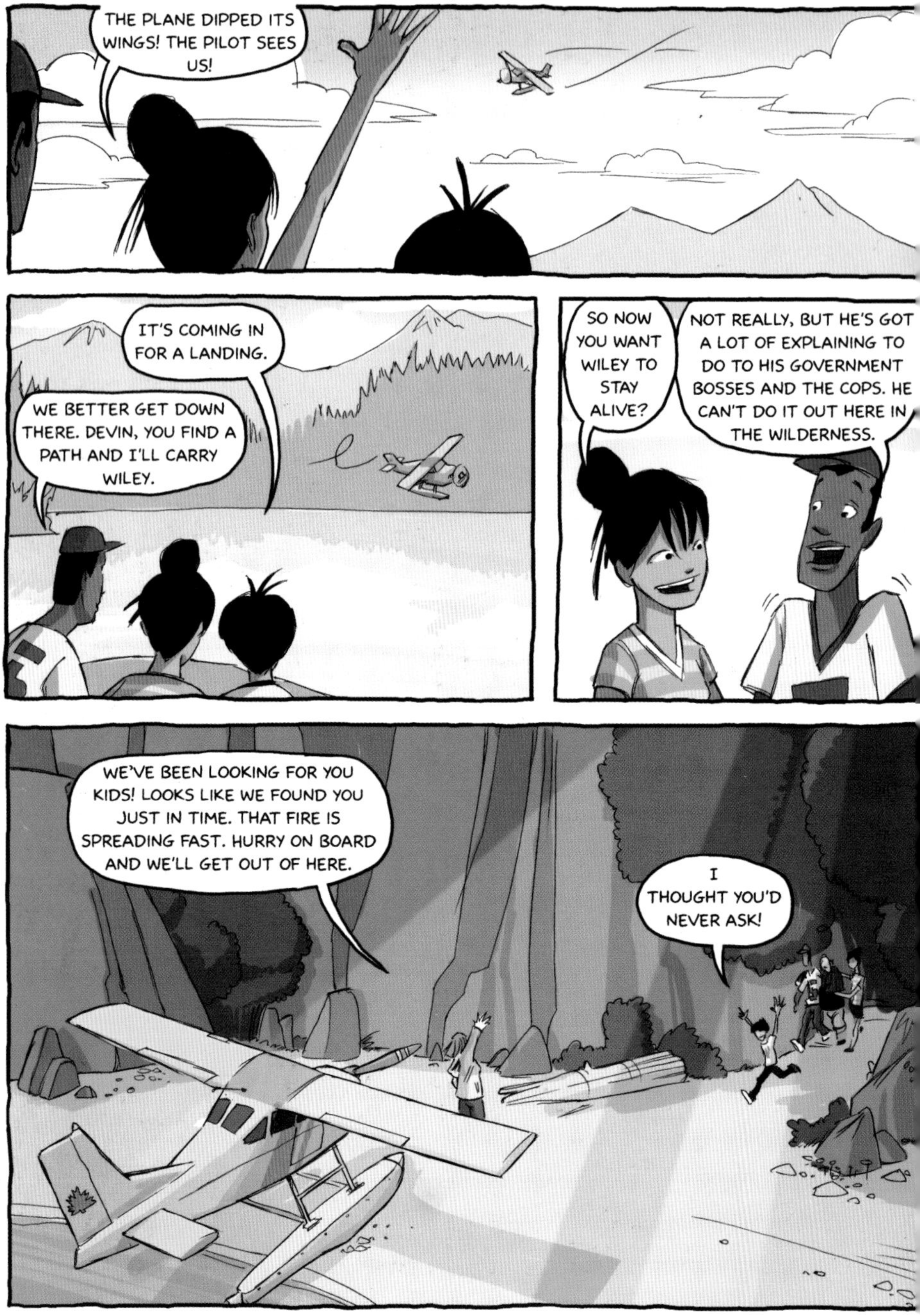
THE PLANE DIPPED ITS WINGS! THE PILOT SEES US!
IT'S COMING IN FOR A LANDING.
WE BETTER GET DOWN THERE. DEVIN, YOU FIND A PATH AND I'LL CARRY WILEY.
SO NOW YOU WANT WILEY TO STAY ALIVE?
NOT REALLY, BUT HE'S GOT A LOT OF EXPLAINING TO DO TO HIS GOVERNMENT BOSSES AND THE COPS. HE CAN'T DO IT OUT HERE IN THE WILDERNESS.
WE'VE BEEN LOOKING FOR YOU KIDS! LOOKS LIKE WE FOUND YOU JUST IN TIME. THAT FIRE IS SPREADING FAST. HURRY ON BOARD AND WE'LL GET OUT OF HERE.
I THOUGHT YOU'D NEVER ASK!

MOM SAYS ONCE THE WILD GETS INSIDE YOU, IT NEVER LEAVES. WE'VE BEEN BACK FOR TWO MONTHS AND THE WILDERNESS IS STILL FRESH IN MY MIND. WHEN I SEE THOSE JERKS WHO PICKED ON ME LAST YEAR, I DON'T RUN. I THINK OF THAT GRIZZLY ON EAGLE PEAK AND STAND MY GROUND.

NADIA DOESN'T TALK ABOUT OUR WILD RIDE MUCH, BUT I KNOW THE WILDERNESS IS IN HER TOO. SHE LAUGHS MORE. SHE TREATS ME DIFFERENTLY. NOT LIKE HER BABY BROTHER. MORE LIKE A FRIEND, I GUESS.

MARCUS IS ONLINE. HE WANTS YOU TO SEE SOMETHING.

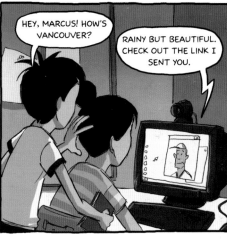

HEY, MARCUS! HOW'S VANCOUVER?

RAINY BUT BEAUTIFUL. CHECK OUT THE LINK I SENT YOU.

CLICK

CNEWS

Scandal saves Big Horn Valley from logging.

In a stunning victory for the environmental group Habitat First, paper giant Klomox & Nash (K&N) was found guilty of bribing government official Gerald Wiley for logging contracts to the pristine northern BC valley.

Evidence given by three youths, Devin and Nadia Chang and Marcus Ashmore, son of Habitat Watch founder Dr. Stanley Ashmore, uncovered plans by K&N to sabotage environmental assessments underway in the valley.

Gerald Wiley has been removed from his government position and faces time in prison when the judge hands down his sentence next week. K&N has already been banned from all logging activities in the province and will likely have to pay large fines to the government.

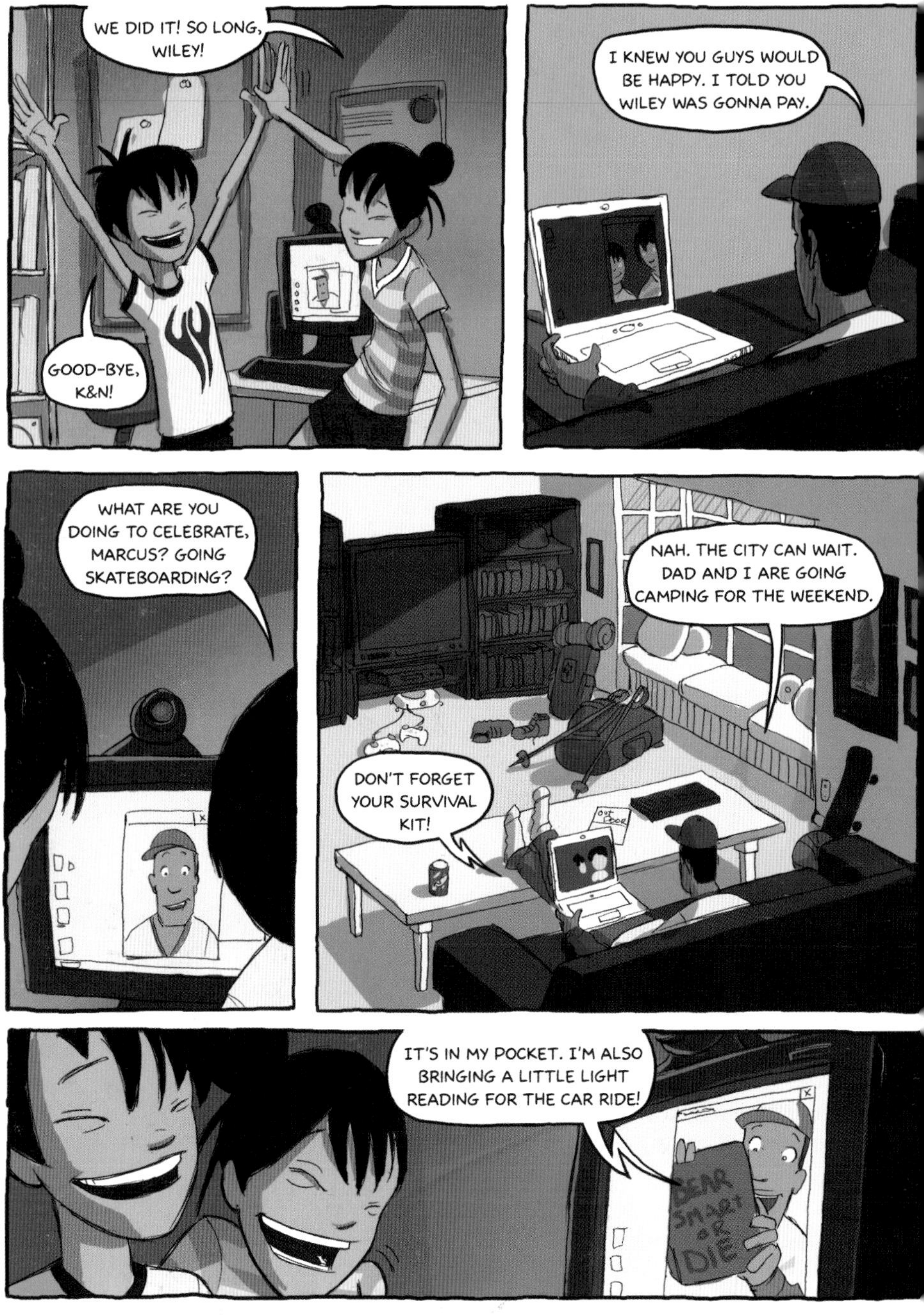
WE DID IT! SO LONG, WILEY!
GOOD-BYE, K&N!
I KNEW YOU GUYS WOULD BE HAPPY. I TOLD YOU WILEY WAS GONNA PAY.
WHAT ARE YOU DOING TO CELEBRATE, MARCUS? GOING SKATEBOARDING?
NAH. THE CITY CAN WAIT. DAD AND I ARE GOING CAMPING FOR THE WEEKEND.
DON'T FORGET YOUR SURVIVAL KIT!
IT'S IN MY POCKET. I'M ALSO BRINGING A LITTLE LIGHT READING FOR THE CAR RIDE!
DEAR SMART OR DIE

*Look for the next installment in the
Graphic Guides Adventure series:*

A GRAPHIC GUIDE ADVENTURE

READ THE ADVENTURE. LEARN THE TRICKS. BE A SKATER.

Fresh from his adventures in *Wild Ride*, Marcus is back and helping his cousin, Bounce, learn to skateboard. Between learning how to ollie and do a 50-50 grind, Bounce and his friends also have to avoid the skate-park goons and take on the outlaw bikers who are terrorizing the small town.

Excitement, action and some radical skating tips. Hang on for another wild ride!

COMING FALL 2008!

WRITTEN BY	ILLUSTRATED BY
LIAM O'DONNELL	**MIKE DEAS**

ABOUT THE AUTHOR

FROM CHAPTER BOOKS TO COMIC STRIPS, LIAM O'DONNELL WRITES FICTION AND NON-FICTION FOR YOUNG READERS. HE IS THE AUTHOR OF THE POPULAR "MAX FINDER MYSTERIES." LIAM LIVES IN TORONTO, ONTARIO.

ABOUT THE ILLUSTRATOR

MIKE DEAS IS A TALENTED ILLUSTRATOR IN A NUMBER OF DIFFERENT GENRES. HE GRADUATED FROM CAPILANO COLLEGE'S COMMERCIAL ANIMATION PROGRAM AND HAS WORKED AS A GAME DEVELOPER. MIKE LIVES IN VICTORIA, BRITISH COLUMBIA.